Coulson Kernahan

**A Dead Man's Diary**

Written after his decease

Coulson Kernahan

**A Dead Man's Diary**
*Written after his decease*

ISBN/EAN: 9783337013059

Printed in Europe, USA, Canada, Australia, Japan

Cover: Foto ©Andreas Hilbeck / pixelio.de

More available books at **www.hansebooks.com**

# A Dead Man's Diary

## Written after his Decease.

WITH A PREFACE BY

## G. T. BETTANY, M.A.

"I sent my Soul through the Invisible,
  Some letter of that After Life to spell:
And by-and-by my Soul return'd to me,
And answered, 'I myself am Heav'n and Hell.'"
RUBÁIYÁT OF OMAR KHAYYÁM.<br>(Fitzgerald's Translation.)

WARD, LOCK AND CO.,
LONDON, NEW YORK AND MELBOURNE.
1890.

# PREFACE.

THE literature purporting to describe the state of mankind after death, whether as Hades, Intermediate State, Purgatory, Hell, or Heaven, has mostly erred in the direction of too great detail. On the one hand, we have had those who with Swedenborg declare "that after death a man is so little changed that he even does not know but he is living in the present world; that the resemblances between the two worlds are so great, that in the spiritual world there are cities, with palaces and houses, and also writings and books, employments and merchandises." On the other hand, we have the picture drawn by the writer of "Letters from Hell," of imaginary houses and scenes, of seeming actions, of semblances of men compelled to appear to be doing after death the very things they did in life, despair all the while gnawing at their hearts. Archdeacon Farrar, in Chapter IV. of his "Mercy and Judgment," has given a varied and horrifying series of extracts from ancient and modern divines describing their detailed conceptions about the future of the wicked. As to the future of the beatified, no one needs reminding of the multitude of word-pictures, often mutually contradictory, in which their existence has been depicted.

Thus we see that the human mind cannot choose but speculate in some fashion on the future state, while no man has the right to claim that he had said the last word on the subject. It may therefore be confidently anticipated that the remarkable narrative here presented, of which considerable portions have already appeared, serially, in the English edition of "Lippincott's Monthly Magazine," will find a very large number of interested readers, who will be glad to peruse it in the connected and completed form, in which it is best calculated to express the author's full meaning and experiences. It will not by its length or excess of detail overburden the reader, nor does it claim to be more than a narrative of experience which may be left to convey its own lessons. The writer, who prefers to remain anonymous, is one whose essays and stories have been received with high appreciation on both sides of the Atlantic. His narrative is put forth as his actual experience during a lengthened absence from the body, during which he was believed to be dead. Of course no other living person can confirm or deny his experiences, though many may deem them incredible, fictitious, or the imaginings or visions of a trancelike state. I do not pretend to decide to what category they belong, nor do I feel called upon to condemn or approve any of the assertions or opinions thus put forward. If any one holds theological convictions which appear to conflict with them, I would remark that the publishers, in letting the " Dead Man " speak for himself, do not hold themselves responsible for his opinions, merely having assured themselves of the serious spirit in which they are narrated.

The record of these experiences being given in the form of a diary, the writer has not felt bound to tell his story with the simple directness which is expected in a work of fiction, but has noted down in his narrative, as is the manner of diarists, the thoughts which the record of his experiences have aroused. Though these occasional digressions have no immediate bearing upon the facts recorded, they will, I think, be found to contain some interesting reading, nor do they, in my opinion, interfere seriously with the completeness of the narrative as an artistic whole.

In conclusion, I would add that the writer only desires that his experiences may be read in a candid spirit, and that as no man can prove him to be wrong who has not actually entered the world of spirits, those who reject his narrative will endeavour to maintain an attitude of suspended judgment, until they are in a position to judge for themselves. For myself, I can but say that the moral of the author's teaching is worthy of the most serious attention, and if put into practice there can be no question that it would conduce greatly to the happiness of mankind.

G. T. BETTANY.

# CONTENTS.

*CONTENTS.*

# CHAPTER I.

## *EXPLAINS MY TITLE.*

IT has always been a favourite fancy of mine that I should like to die upon some sunny, songful morning, in spring or early summer. The thought of dying in the night, and of finding this thin and aërial something, which I have learned to call "my soul," being driven remorselessly nightward, as Adam and Eve were driven from Paradise; the seeing it in imagination, a spectral, unsubstantial shadow of myself, flitting a-shivering out into the black-wombed darkness, and fumbling with filmy hands that it might clasp the closer around it the warm familiar robe of flesh, only to find that robe fallen away for ever—this thought, I must confess, fills me at all times with an abhorrent loathing and dread.

To look up by night at the cold glitter of the stars, and to fancy my disembodied spirit winging its weary way thereto, through fathomless leagues of void and voiceless ether, causes me ever to shiver, and to turn shudderingly to earth again ; but the thought of passing peacefully away upon some sunny, summer morning seems less like dying than like stepping out of doors to be among the birds and the butterflies. *Then* the heaven of my hopes would not seem so very distant after all (and oh ! how much more heavenly and homelike would that heaven appear did I but know it to be *this* side of the stars !), and my first entry into the dim and shadowy realm of the spirit-world would seem the less strange and unfamiliar for my having to pass out on my way to it through the fields, the flowers, and the sunshine that I love so well.

To me, however, in the utter solitude of midnight waking, and in the scarcely less utter solitude of day-dreaming in the midst of men, the thought which ever most oppresses me in the contemplation of death, is not so much the Unknown which lies beyond, as the thought of its awful loneliness,—the thought that human faces may shine on my face, human hands lie clasped in mine, and human voices bear me company up to the very boundary line of that still and silent land, but that when that boundary line is once reached, all these must fail and forsake me, and I must turn to face the unknown darkness naked, desolate, and alone.

But why do I allow my thoughts, you say, to brood thus morbidly upon death and the death moment ? I will tell you. Because I who now write to you have—save only in the last and uttermost giving up of the spirit —been for some narrow space of time dead ; because on me there once fell that thin and impalpable veil which cuts off, as by a wall of vast and impenetrable night, the dead one from those whom he leaves behind.

The facts of the matter are simply these. Some years ago I became seriously ill, grew worse day by day, and was pronounced dying, and finally dead. Dead I apparently was, and dead I remained to all intents and purposes for the greater part of two days, after which, to the intense and utter astonishment of my friends and of the physicians, I exhibited symptoms of returning vitality, and in the course of a week or two was convalescent. The medical and scientific aspects of the case are, I am assured by those most competent to judge, of unusual interest, but it is not to them that I now wish to direct attention. It is rather to that dim borderland betwixt life and death, wherein the spirit hovers on uncertain pinion, as if hesitating whether to return to the body it has lately tenanted, or to wing its way to the shadowy heights of the world Unseen.

Where, during those two-score hours, I would ask, was my soul, ghost, or life-principle? Had it passed into some inter-mediate spirit-realm, there to await till the Father of Spirits should command it either finally to quit the mortal habitation in which it had so long found a home, or to return thereto till such time as He should call it to Himself? Or was it still hovering over the

B

body, struggling and striving to free itself
from the fetters which bound it to that which,
without it, were but a senseless and inani-
mate clod ?

To that question I am prepared with an
answer, and so strange a one, that I cannot
hope my story will be regarded with anything but incredulity, nor can I reasonably
expect it to be otherwise, for I am aware
that what I am about to relate I myself
should reject unhesitatingly were it proffered
me on the testimony of another.

# CHAPTER II.

### DEALS WITH DEATH AND THE DREAD OF IT.

IF the thoughts which are coursing through my brain at this moment be not less gruesome to read than they are to write, this chapter will, I fear, be but sorry reading; for I feel strangely depressed and nervous, as I settle down to the opening pages of my diary.

The wind is raging and roaring outside until the stout walls of the house seem to rock and sway like tree-tops, and the sudden gusts and squalls make my startled heart

bound and beat faster in my bosom, and
turn me sick with a sense of loneliness and
of loss.

Even when I lie warm in my bed the
sound of the wind at midnight strikes a
chill through me, so that I shiver in spite
of the blankets. As it comes shrieking and
sobbing through key-hole and lattice, the
very doors and windows seem to partake of
my superstition, and to be touched with
some uncanny dread ; for long after it has
died away I hear them creaking complain-
ingly among themselves, as if they too were
nervous and in fear. In the wind's shriek
at such times there is always to me some
suggestion of the sights it has seen, and of
the ruin it has wrought. I seem to see, as I
listen to its wailing, a weary moon that looks
out white and wan upon a bleak heath,
where a dead woman lies straining a living

babe to her milkless breast ; or upon a waste of hurrying waters that heave and roar and hurl themselves in huge billows upon one desolate figure, clinging despairingly to a broken mast. And then there is a sudden lull in the storm ; the moon is hidden by clouds once more, and the infant's wail, the strong man's cry, and the shriek of the wind, gloating in savage exultation over its ghastly secrets, die away into a distant rumble, and all is still save the beating of my heart, and the stealthy creaking of door and casement.

Even as I write I can hear its wailing so die away in the distance, and I seem to see it crouching, still and quiet and panther-like, yet ever gathering itself together, and creeping nearer and nearer, so that it may take me unaware, and in one sudden bound sweep down upon me, as an eagle swoops upon his prey, and bear me away to destruction.

Listen to it now !—whistling, wailing, shrieking, like a live thing ! Is it any wonder, on such a night, and with a sound in the air like that of innumerable lamentations, that I feel strangely conscious of the near approach of death, and cannot dissociate my thoughts from

" The knell, the shroud, the mattock, and the grave,
   The deep damp vault, the darkness, and the worm." ?

For I *do* fear death, as I believe we all do in some moods. Notwithstanding our reiterated beliefs in Christ and in Immortality; notwithstanding our prayers, hymn-singing, and heartfelt declarations of our trust in God, and in His care for us, are there not moments in the life of each of us when the human nature within recoils in dumb and desolate protest from the thought of an existence in which the body will be left to decay ? We think at such times of our own death and burial. We picture the mourning coaches setting out, with solemn pomp and pageantry of woe, to bear us away to our last earthly resting-place. We see them drive back — briskly now, and as though the grief were left behind with the coffin—to the darkened house, and we see the mourners alight and re-enter to draw up the blinds with a sigh of thinly-disguised satisfaction, and to turn with a natural if humiliating relief to life and the things of life again. And as we think of the darkness coming on, and of that deserted body of ours, which had once so craved for light and warmth and human companionship, lying, in the first awful night of desolation, away out under the sods in that dreary cemetery, we can almost fancy that we see the uneasy soul, restless even in heaven, stealing sadly to earth again, and hovering, for very companionship, over the forsaken mound that covers its ancient comrade.

So, too, there are moments of midnight waking, when we lie on our bed as in a grave, and feel the awful thought of death borne in upon us with unutterable, intolerable horror. Then the darkness which shuts out those objects that in the day-time distract the attention of our outward eye, and of our mind, serves only to make our mental vision doubly keen, and to concentrate all our faculties, as to one inward focal point of light, on that hateful thought. Then do we seem to feel the earth rushing swiftly on its way, as if eager to hurry us to our own dissolution; and then do we stretch forth impotent hands and vain, striving hopelessly to stay it on its course. Yet ever is our striving of none avail : Death, hideous and inexorable, stares us in the face—a wall of

vast and impenetrable night, which closes in
upon us on every side. We gasp and choke
as though some bony and cruel fingers lay
clutching at our throat. "Is there no way,"
we cry, with heart strained unto bursting,
"is there no way by which we may escape
the Inescapable? — no loop-hole through
which we may creep, and elude this black
and grisly thing?" But from the hollow
womb of night comes back the sullen answer,
"Escape there is none," and then, like
doomed criminals who snatch greedily at a
day's reprieve, we thrust the ghastly thing
away from us, and strive to distract our
thoughts in folly.

# CHAPTER III.

## DEALS WITH LIFE AND THE LUST OF IT, BUT HAS NO DIRECT BEARING ON MY STORY.*

Shall we not weary in the windless days
    Hereafter, for the murmur of the sea,
    The cool salt air across some grassy lea?
Shall we not go bewildered through a maze
Of stately streets with glittering gems ablaze,
    Forlorn amid the pearl and ivory,
    Straining our eyes beyond the bourne to see
Phantoms from out life's dear forsaken ways?

---

\* Then why print it here? asks the reader. For the reason, I reply, that this Diary is the history, not only of a sin, but of a soul; and that to leave the aspect of my subject here treated unnoticed would be to give but a maimed and one-sided representation. I do not think any reader who studies my sketch-outline as a whole will consider the introduction of this chapter as inartistic.

Give us again the crazy clay-built nest,
    Summer, and soft unseasonable spring,
    Our flowers to pluck, our broken songs to sing,
Our fairy gold of evening in the West ;
    Still to the land we love our longings cling,
The sweet vain world of turmoil and unrest.
                  —GRAHAM R. TOMSON.

LET me frankly confess that I love this world and the things of it, and so, I believe, do all in whom the "great, glad, aboriginal" and God-given love of life is whole and healthy, and not stunted by sickness of mind or body. For the bereaved and the sorrow-stricken I make every allowance and would have all tenderness, but I suspect either the honesty or the health (and by "health" I mean, of course, mental as well as physical soundness) of those who express themselves as being "desirous of departing," or who assert that love of this world is irreconcilable with the love of God.

It is not God's world, with its love and friendship and little children, its fields and flowers, sea and sky, sunlight and starshine, and sweet consolations of Art and Song, against which we are bidden to beware. No it is *man's* world—the world which devotes itself to gain, or to the wish to be somebody in society; to the frittering away of our days in fashionable frivolity, or in struggling to outdo our neighbour, not in the purity of our lives, or the dignity of our actions, but in our clothes, our carriages, and the company we keep—*this* world it is which cannot be rightly loved by one in whom dwelleth the love of the Father.

But God's world we can never love half enough, can never sufficiently appreciate and enjoy. Suppose that you and I, my reader, had to make a world—call it a heaven if you will—of our own designing, and were entrusted with infinite potentialities for the purpose. Could we, could all of us combined, ever conceive of anything half so beautiful as this world at which so many of us gaze with apathetic eyes ?

> " An idle poet, here and there,
>     Looks round him, but for all the rest,
>   The world, unfathomably fair,
>     Is duller than a witling's jest."

At best we could but copy, but if it so happened that we, to whom it was given to create, had never been permitted to set eyes even upon this earth beforehand, what sort of a world then, think you, should we contrive to construct ?

I believe that if God were to make a man, a full-grown man in a moment, and were to set him down in the midst of the world, to

look upon it with new eyes, and for the first
time, instead of letting him grow up from a
child, *to become accustomed to it*—for it is
true, as Mr. Lowell says, that "we glance
carelessly at the sunrise, and get used to
Orion and the Pleiades,"—I believe that that
man would be in danger of delirium from
his overwhelming joy and wonder at the
beauty and the boundlessness of that which
he saw around.

Even this grim old London is full of
beauty and of boundlessness; of beauty
which strikes me breathless, and of boundlessness of life, and sky; for in what slum
of it, be it never so stifling, are we quite
shut out from view of the stars or the
sunshine, or of the human faces that come
and go in the streets? But a moment ago,
while looking out from my window upon
a crowded, choking city thoroughfare, I

caught one glimpse of a woman's profile, as
she passed with her head poised, and half-
turned towards me; and though the vision
was gone in an instant, the sweep of the
queenly neck, ivory-white and stately as a
lily-stem, set my senses vibrating with a
thrill of exquisite pleasure. And yonder,
looking into a window, I see another face,
the sweet pure face of a maiden. I run my
eye like a finger along the profile, I follow
the flowing line of the hair; but even as I
look, she turns, is gone and is forgotten, for
her place is taken by a girl with a basket
of flowers, the flowers that I love as I love
nothing else but poetry. It is Emerson, I
think, who tells us that God's loveliest gifts
are the commonest; and that sun and sky
and flowers are scarce denied to a beggar's
call; and it is pitiful, as he says in another
passage, the things by which we call our-

selves rich or poor. Why, I have gone
home from my morning's walk, feeling richer
in the possession of a handful of honey-
suckle than if I had found a purse of
sovereigns by the wayside ; nor could all the
art-treasures of Bond Street (not that I fail
to appreciate them, either) give me a more
exquisite thrill of sweetly-saddened pleasure
than does the tender perfume of a bunch of
violets.

As a child I used to fancy that I found in
a flower all my whitest and purest thoughts
crystallized into a thing ; and now, though I
am a man, the white-pure thoughts of my
childhood still live for me in every flower
that blossoms in the meadows ; for the
flowers bring me back not only my vanished
childhood, but my childhood's innocence and
peace. Even in those remote child-days I
was persuaded that the flowers were not of

earth, but of heaven, nor while I had them could I believe heaven to be so very far off, after all. " Else how could the flower-seeds have been blown over its edge, and fallen down to the earth-land ? " I would say to myself. And I find myself fancying now, as I fancied then, that God takes the flowers home to His heaven in the winter, and every spring when I welcome them back, I feel that they have come as direct from Him and from heaven as if He had leant down out of the skies to give them to me; and I feel that they are not my flowers, but His flowers ; for even as I gather them to call them mine, He puts forth His hand and claims them, so that they fade away again to the heaven whence they came.

Yes, I love this world, and the things of it. To me the mere consciousness of life is a gladness, the pulsing of my heart a

C

pleasure. I pencil the latter part of this
chapter while lying lazily in a sun-filled
meadow, and as I write I seem to feel the
very drawing of my breath a joy. The sky
spreads above me, a shimmering sea of blue
—not the cool, crystalline sapphire of early
morning, but the deep dense azure of a mid-
summer noon. How hot the bees must feel
in that furry coat! As I lie here, basking
in the sunlight, and watching the buttercups
dancing and dipping above the grass, like
golden banners amid an army of green-
bladed bayonets, I do not wonder that the
poor bees keep up a dull droning hum of
monotonous murmuring. I can see the hot
air simmering and quivering above the
clover fields, but all else is drowsily,
dreamily still. I know that the streets of
the far-off city are reeking and smoking
with dry and dusty heat, but here I am in

another world, and the bees and the birds are my brothers. This meadow is my boundless prairie ; my head is below the level of the grass tops, and they spread feathery, filmy arms above, like the boughs of a vast forest.

Yes, lying here in this sun-filled meadow on this summer morning, I am conscious that I love my life, and that I should be loath to leave it. I love to feel the wind upon my cheek, and to hear it as it whistles by me, singing in my ears, as in the hollow con-volutions of a shell. I love to stand and look out upon the sea, or upon open plains and broad sky-spaces, which give us *eyesight room* and room for our souls to be. I love to lie and listen to the song of the wind among the pine-trees,—the " sailing " pine trees,—and to watch them swing and sway like storm-tossed barks at sea. I love to

see the rook beat up against the wind, and
poise and hover and soar, and slide down
upon the edge of the blast with rigid blade-
like wings that shear the air like a knife.
And when I watch him cut the ether in
circles as full and fair as the curves of a
woman's bosom, I think of him less as a bird
than as some winged artist of the heights,
who delights in flowing line, and grace of
form and feature ; and I too feel buoyant
and airy, and to my very limbs is lent the
lightness of his flight.

I love, too, the companionship of those
who love the things that I love—my
spiritual brethren and fellow-worshippers ;
for, to my thinking, the lovers of Art, Music,
Nature, Poetry, or of Religion, are all of
them in one attitude of mind, and are animated by one and the same spirit—I call it
the Worshipping Spirit. It may body itself

forth in the homage-love of the musician for harmony, in the artist-worship of sensuous beauty, or, highest of all, in the adoration of Christ and of that which is spiritually perfect; and yet all these loves are not many loves, but one love, for they are but different expressions of one and the same spirit. Hence to turn from a chapter of St. John to a sunset, a sonnet from Wordsworth, or a picture by Botticelli, is to me not unseemly, but natural, for each of these arouses, in different degrees, one and the same emotion, and that emotion has its source in one and the same Worshipping Spirit.

I love also travel, change and adventure. I love the Botticellis, the Fra Angelicos and the Leonardo of our own princely National Gallery, not the less, but the better for an occasional ramble in the Louvre, or among the galleries of Holland or Italy. I love

the life, the stir and bustle of our London
streets ; but I love, too, the old-world rest
and repose of Bruges or of Berne ; and many
a time have I lingered the long day through
in the antique streets of Antwerp, listening
to the sweet uproar and silvern wrangling
that ripples, cloud-borne and wind-wafted,
from where the stately belfry soars lark-like
above the world.    To me to have been
happy once is to establish a claim upon
happiness thenceforward, and. it is for this
reason, I suppose, that I love so to re-live
the past, and to dwell on the memory of
former sights and scenes.    It is true, as
Frederick Robertson says, that the " first
time never returns," and shall I ever forget
the exultation of the moment when, after
repeated failures, I first set foot on that inaccessible mountain-height which I had
risked my life to scale?    Even now, lying

here in this sunny English meadow, I seem to re-live that moment, and to see that scene again. Before me rises one wild and wasteful world of white—a white on which the fierce rays of the sun beat and burn with blinding, blazing, intolerable brilliance. Above, swimming and soaring away into unfathomable azure, spreads the silent heaven, but around, about, beneath, all is white, deathly-white, save only where the vast angles of ice-crag or column deepen into a lustrous turquoise, or where a blue mist broods athwart the mouth of yawning crevasse or cavern. Below me and afar—so far that it seems as if I were cut off from it for ever,—lies the sunny village that I left so many toilsome hours ago, just visible, a wee white dot upon the green. There the air is sweet with the breath of flowers and of the clover-fields, there, too, are the bees,

and the butterflies, and the music of rushing
water. But here, where the wasteful snows
writhe and wreathe around in arch and cave
and column, vast and wonderful to behold—
above, the shining zenith, below, the sheer
abyss and the treacherous descent—here in
the solemn solitude and silence of this
whited wilderness, I can scarcely believe
that I am still on the earth, and of it, and
that the dazzling dome on which I am
standing is but the white and swelling bosom
of the Great Mother from whom we all
sprang.

Or, weary of the silence and the snow-
solitudes, I close my eyes, and lo! I am
down in the valley again, and all around me
spreads a blithe and beauteous scene of
serenest summer. On every breeze that
sings from sunny slope or smiling pasture is
borne the windy chime and clamour of

countless cattle-bells from the hillside, but beyond that, and the unbroken *buzz* and *burr*, which bespeak the deep content of innumerable bees, all is still, drowsily still. Here, if anywhere, one can realize for a moment the deep, dreamy peacefulness that pervades the opening lines of Mr. Swinburne's majestic " Garden of Proserpine,"—

> " Here, where the world is quiet,
>     Here, where all trouble seems
> Dead winds' and spent waves' riot
>     In doubtful dream of dreams ;
> I watch the green field growing,
> For reaping folk and sowing,
> For harvest time and mowing,
>     A sleepy world of streams."

Here are the bees, the birds, and the butterflies ; here, too, nestling cosily on hillside or meadow, are dotted dozens of umber-brown châlets, each of which seems to suggest that "haunting sense of human

history " of which George Macdonald speaks,
when he says that " many a simple home
will move one's heart like a poem, many a
cottage like a melody."

And now there is a change in the picture :
the drowsiness and the dreaminess are gone,
and there is the free, fresh sense of motion,
and of the open. In my ears is the journeying music of the *diligence*—music which
despite its jingle never becomes monotonous,
for every now and then the horses toss their
heads to shake off the too persistent flies,
and sprinkle the air with spray of silvery
sounds. The road winds along a mountain
path overlooking a lake, and the mirroring of
sunset fire upon the surface of the water, the
cool clear crystal of the blue depths that
swim away below, the purple distance of the
farther hills, fast-shrouding in light-drawn
mist, and lastly, the solemn splendour of that

sky-hung, soaring summit, brooding like a presence athwart the skies,—all these make up a scene upon which I am never weary of dwelling, and which I dearly love to recall; a scene of such indescribable loveliness as to leave me at last bowed and breathless, and

"Sad with the whole of pleasure."

I thought when I penned the last para-graph that I had made an end of telling you of my love of life and of the things of it, but that half-line which I have quoted from Rossetti's most beautiful sonnet sets me thinking of another love of which I have not yet spoken. Need I say that I mean the love of music? not only of the music which is "like soft hands stealing into ours in the dark, and holding us fast without a spoken word," but also of those sobbing soaring strains, which sound as sadly in our ears as does the wintry flittering of dead leaves upon

a withered bough ? To those who feel that
every ray of morning sunlight which strikes
across their path calls them to a higher and
holier living ; to whose hearts the pure petals
of a primrose are as a silent reproach against
their own impurity ; to whom a glint of blue
sky, gleaming out between rain-beaten tree-
tops is as an aspiration towards a loftier,
lovelier life ; to whom the very wind, as it
sings from the gates of morning, cries out
"Unclean! unclean!"—to such, I suppose,
music must ever contain less of joy than
of sadness, if, indeed, it appeal not with a
pleasure which cuts to the heart like a pain.
It is to them as if an angel from heaven
had cast, for one passing second, upon a
cloud-screen drawn across the soul, a vision
of what they *might* be, of what they were
*meant* to be, and of what in God's good
time they may yet become; and as if at

the very moment when the spirit was pouring itself forth in one unutterable cry of
longing after the Divine beauty of that ideal,
there rose before them the shadow-horror of
what they really are.

# CHAPTER IV.

## *I DIE.*

I PASS on now to tell of my death moments. The room in which I died was the room in which I had been born. One half of it was my bedroom, and the other half—that near the window—was my study. There I had done all my work, and there were my books and papers. There, too, grouped around the walls, were portraits of the men and women who seem to me sometimes to be more myself, as Emerson puts it, than even I am, and who are nearer to me and dearer to me, many of them, than

arc some ot those who sit daily with me
in the household—I mean the portraits of
my favourite writers.

I do not know whether the literary associ-
ations of the room had any part—probably
they had—in determining the current of my
thought, but I remember that, during the
first few hours of the morning preceding
my death, I found my mind running on
poets and poetry. I recollect that I was
thinking chiefly of Rossetti, and of the fact
that he was haunted, as he lay a-dying, by
passages from his own poems. Not that I
saw or see any cause in that fact for wonder,
for I can recall lines of his which I can
believe would haunt one even in heaven.

Those of my readers who fail to appreciate in its fulness the saying of " Diana
of the Crossways " that in poetry " those
that have souls meet their fellows," or that

of the *Saturday Review*, that "there is an
incommunicable magic in poetry which is
foolishness to the multitude,"—may think
this an exaggeration.    Ah well, they are
of the " multitude,"—the more pity for them !
—and can never understand how the soul
is stirred by a simple sentence in the god-
like language of Shakespeare, or is as irresistibly swayed as are trees in a whirlwind
by a single stanza from Swinburne; how
the magic witchery of a couplet by Keats
can bring tears to the eyes; or how the
tender grace of a line from Herrick can set
the senses vibrating with an exquisite thrill
of joy.    Nay, I could indicate sentences in
the diamond-pointed prose of George Meredith, pellucid sentences, crystal-clear and
luminous as the scintillations of Sirius (and
for all their judicial poise and calmness
emitted like the Sirius scintillations at a

white heat),—which affect me in a similar way. There are few other writers of whom I could affirm this with the like confidence; but Meredith's thoughts have crystallized into a brain-stimulating prose—every sentence of which is a satisfying mouthful to our intellectual hunger—which is sometimes pure poetry.

Poetry is to my diary, however, and in fact to all I think or say, what King Charles's head was to Mr. Dick's memorial, and it is time I returned to my narrative.

The possibility of a fatal ending to my illness had never occurred to myself or to my family, until that ending was nigh at hand, and so it was that death came upon me in every way unawares. I remember my father bending over me, and asking gently if I knew that I was dying, and I recollect looking up to whisper back, " No :

D

is it so?" and receiving his sorrowful re-
sponse. It was too late then for me to do
more than recognise the fact as a fact, for
my brain was so strangely affected that I
was utterly incapable of following out that
fact to its result. I knew that I was dying
—knew it much as I might have known it
of some other person—but felt no individual
pang of terror or surprise. This state ot
indifferent acquiescence in that which was
about to occur was followed by a sense of
regret at having to leave a volume which I
had in hand unfinished, and then, with the
ruling passion strong in death, I found myself endeavouring to find fitting words to
describe my sensations. It is so with me
ever and always. Art and Poetry have become such realities, that I cannot take them
up and lay them aside at pleasure, but must
needs bear them with me whithersoever I

go. I carry my poetry with me to bed and
to breakfast; and I can sit and write, or
carry on a conversation, with the consciousness of Mr. Lang's latest *Ballade*, or Mr.
Theodore Watts's last sonnet, running like
an undercurrent in my mind. I am perpetually striving to fix in language the fleet-
ing colours of sea and sky. I can never
listen to the trickle and purl of a brooklet
tinkling over its pebbly bed, without making
diligent search in my vocabulary for a word
—the golden word—which seems most to
babble and to blab of water. As surely as
I find in Wordsworth's poems a background
of sky and mountain, just as surely do I
find in mountain and sky an echo of Wordsworth's song. To me, too, the sonnet which
rises involuntarily to my lips, as I gaze out
upon the deep, is as much a part of the
scene before me, as is the sun or the sand

upon the shore; and I have come to feel with Mr. Lowell, as if a sunset were "like a quotation from Dante or Milton," and that "if Shakespeare be read in the very presence of the sea itself, his voice shall but seem nobler for the sublime criticism of ocean." .

I was telling you that as I lay a-dying, I found myself endeavouring to find fitting words to describe my sensations. At this point, however, the train of my thoughts was disturbed—and I recollect a slight re-awakening of my old characteristic irritability at the interruption—by the entrance of a sister who had come from a distance to see me. I remember slightly lifting my head to speak to her, and then glancing round the room to see if all were present. Yes, close beside me, and with his head bowed over his hands, sat my father, and

round about the bed were gathered the remainder of the family. Nor were these all,
for standing among them were three other
figures—that of my brother Fred, whose
grave as yet was hardly green, and of my
mother and my little sister Comfort, both
of whom had died when I was a child.
If my conviction that I have indeed been
dead be a delusion,—as I doubt not many
of my readers will think,—is it not strange,
I would ask, that these faces should have
been with me at the end? Had there been
any conjecture in my mind as to the probability of my meeting with my lost ones,
I could readily believe that what I saw
was the creation of my own brain. But
there had been no such conjecture, for death
had taken me, as I have already explained,
entirely unawares, and no thought of the
dead had as much as occurred to me.

Their presence, however, so far from caus-
ing me any surprise, seemed perfectly
natural, for the fact that they were dead
did not dawn upon my consciousness.

This, I am ready to allow, strongly sup-
ports the theory that these experiences
may be nothing more than dreams, for in
dreams it not seldom happens that we re-
live the past, and hold converse with our
departed ones, all oblivious of the death
which has come between us. It *may* be
so, I admit, but in my heart of hearts I
cannot think it ; for if all that I have to
tell be but a dream, then does it seem to
me the strangest dream ever dreamed by
man. Moreover, with these three figures
was a fourth—a figure which at first had
escaped my notice ; and it is the presence
of this figure in the room which is to me
most unaccountable. My mother, when I

first saw her, was standing at the foot of the bed, with my dead brother and sister looking over her shoulder, but at the sight of my father's grief, she went gently round to where he was sitting, and with a caress of infinite pity stooped down as if to whisper in his ear. It was then that I saw for the first time that she held by the hand a little child—a little child whom I had never seen before, but across whose face, as he looked up at me, there flitted the phantom of a resemblance I could not catch.

I remember that even then, brain-benumbed and dying as I was, I wondered who that little child could be; but there dawned upon me no shadowy suspicion of the truth, and I passed away with that wonder unremoved.

I think now—nay, I am sure—that I know who that child was. It was my brother James John, the eldest of the family, who had died before I was born, and whom, in this world, therefore, I had never seen.

I have little left to tell of my death, for nothing else occurred of any moment, and I am resolved to confine myself strictly to facts. I remember that immediately after I had seen my mother, and while I was wondering who the child she held by the hand could be, there came over me a strange and sudden sense of loss—of physical loss, I think it was, as though some life-element had gone out from me. Of pain there was none, nor was I disturbed by any mental anxiety. I recollect only an ethereal lightness of limb, and a sense of soul-emancipation and peace—a sense of soul-emancipation such as one might feel were he to awaken on a sunny morning to find that all sorrow and sin were gone from the

world for ever; a peace ample and restful
as the hallowed hush and awe of summer
twilight, without the twilight's tender pain.

Then I seemed to be sinking slowly and
steadily through still depths of sun-steeped,
light-filled waters that sang in my ears
with a sound like a sweet-sad sobbing and
soaring of music, and through which there
swam up to me, in watered vistas of light,
scenes of sunny seas and shining shores
where smiling isles stretched league beyond league afar. And so life ebbed and
ebbed away, until at last there came a
time—the moment of death, I believe—
when the outward and deathward setting
tide seemed to reach its climax, and when
I felt myself swept shoreward and lifeward
again on the inward-setting tide of that
larger life into which I had died.

# CHAPTER V.

*IS OF AN EXPLANATORY NATURE ONLY.*

WHEN the first rough draft of this diary was lying on my study table, there called to see me, at a time when I chanced to be out, a certain novelist who is an old and intimate friend of mine. He was shown into the study to await my coming, and, on my return, I found him amusing himself with these papers. Of the reality of my death-experiences (which he persistently refused to regard as other than dreams) I had never been able to convince him, and I was not surprised therefore when, after the conversation turned upon the work each of us had in hand, he referred to my booklet in his usual sceptical tone.

"My dear fellow," he said, laying one hand upon the offending manuscript, " I haven't the slightest intention of disputing the truth of your statements, or of denying that your diary has a certain unwholesome interest of its own, but seriously, I don't think fiction is altogether in your line."

"Nor satire in yours," I replied; "but what have you to say against the thing now?"

"This," he answered, more evidently in earnest, "that you haven't scored as you might have done, but have let slip what opportunities you had for turning out something original. 'Letters from Hell' (which, by the bye, you must expect to be charged

with imitating, though *that* needn't trouble
you much) was confessedly a work of pure
imagination, and I shouldn't be surprised if
the fact helped somewhat to lessen the
interest of the volume. Now your book has
just enough shadow of probability or possibility to sustain the delusion, and all that
will tell in its favour. The public likes—
just as Dick Swiveller's Marchioness did—
to 'make believe' in the reality of that
which is meant to interest it; and books
or plays can't be too life-like or realistic
nowadays. You have 'made believe' until
you have brought yourself to believe in the
reality of something which I can't think
ever happened; but that isn't my business.
What I complain of is this :—that although
you have a story to tell with sufficient
shadow of probability or possibility, as I
have said, to make it interesting, and to

keep up the delusion, you have failed most
lamentably to turn your opportunities to
account. Take your death scene, for
instance. Any practical writer of ordinary
ability could *imagine* the sensations of dying,
and could draw a far more powerful picture
of them than you have done, who profess
to have actually experienced those sensations personally. Then what you have to
say about Heaven and Hell, and all the
rest of it, is curious, and some may think it
not uninteresting, but you haven't given us
any idea of what the places are like, after
all. Why didn't you draw on your imagination, man ? Why didn't you go in for the
grim, and grey, and ghastly ? Why didn't
you revel in the weird (never mind Mr.
Lang's abuse of the word), or conjure up
blissful dreams of the blest and of Paradise ?
I know a dozen men who could have made

twice as much capital, and far more saleable
copy, out of that idea of yours about a
man dying, or nearly so, and then coming
back to relate what he has seen, as it
appears from the standpoint of frail mor-
tality; and I tell you frankly that I don't
think you have scored as you ought to have
done."

" But what has all this," says the reader,
"to do with your diary ? We are willing
to hear what you have to tell about your
experiences, but we didn't bargain for an
article setting forth the opinion of your
friends on the subject, and we can't help
thinking that the introduction of this chapter
is somewhat uncalled for."

Well, perhaps it is so, but it is because
the conversation given above touches upon
some points concerning which I am anxious
that the reader should come to a right

understanding before he enters upon my
after-death experience, that I have inserted
it here, and if a very few minutes' indulgence
be granted me, I will say what I have to say
as briefly as possible. I could, I am sure,
by drawing a little on my imagination, have
written a far more striking description of
the sensations of death, than that which I
have given in the preceding chapter, for of
such description, in the sense of "working-
up a situation" there is absolutely none.
All that I have tried to do is to relate my
story with a resolute avoidance of anything
akin to the sensational. If aught of the
sensational there be in the narrative, it is
because the thing is sensational in itself,
and not because I have attempted to make
it so. As George Eliot says, it is far easier
to draw a griffin, with wings and claws filled
in according to our own fancy, than to

correctly limn the outlines of a lion ; and to keep to the truth has been the hardest part of my task.

When the mental picture or impression left on my mind is but an imperfect one, I have not attempted, as I might easily and perhaps pardonably have done, to fill in the missing outline from my imagination, but have given the picture or impression for what it is worth, and have left it so. My memory is, generally speaking, excellent, and during the first few hours of consciousness after the return of vitality, the recollection of that which I had seen was as fresh as are the events of yesterday. Within a week, however, I found that the greater part of it had gone from me, and that all my efforts to recall the mental pictures were unavailing. I have sometimes wondered if it can be possible that when my presence was missed from the realms into which I had so untimely wandered, some angelic messenger was despatched with instructions to wipe out from the tablets of my memory the records of my experiences. Whether it be so, or not, I cannot say, but this I do know, that had I commenced my diary within a week of my return to life, the booklet would have been one such as it is not often given to man to write. The subject, however, seemed then, and for a long time after, too solemn to be turned to account for "copy," and each of the several years which have elapsed since I died, has taken with it some part of the recollections that remained to me; and now that I have all too tardily set about my task, I have but blurred and broken reminiscences to offer in place of a life-like picture.

These reminiscences, vague, disconnected,

E

and fragmentary as they are, I have given for what they are worth. If any reader think that I have overrated the value of my experiences, and that I have failed to verify the promise with which I started, I can only assure him that the failure is due, not to the insufficiency of what is strange and striking in my experiences, but to my inability to recall what I have seen, and to my incompetency to do fitting justice to my singular subject.

# CHAPTER VI.

*TELLS OF MY FIRST AWFUL AWAKENING
IN HELL, AND OF THE SHAMEFUL SIN
WHICH BROUGHT ME THITHER.*

THE expense of spirit in a waste of shame
    Is lust in action ; and till action, lust
Is perjured, murderous, bloody, full of blame,
    Savage, extreme, rude, cruel, not to trust,
Enjoyed no sooner but despisèd straight,
    Past reason hunted, and no sooner had
Past reason hated, as a swallowed bait,
    On purpose laid to make the taker mad ;
Mad in pursuit, and in possession so ;
    Had, having, and in quest to have, extreme ;
A bliss in proof, and, proved, a very woe ;
    Before, a joy proposed ; behind, a dream.
All this the world well knows ; yet none knows well
To shun the heaven that leads men to this hell.

                *Shakespeare's 129th Sonnet.*

TIME, which is the name we give to our petty portion of Eternity, has no existence in that Eternity which has been defined as the "lifetime of the Almighty"; and so it was that though I remained in the spirit realm but two days, it seemed to me as if weeks, months, years, had elapsed between my death and the hour when I first became conscious of that death.

I have told you that as I lay a-dying, I felt my life slowly but steadily ebbing away, until at last there came a time—the moment of death, I believe it to have been—when the outward and deathward-setting tide seemed to reach its climax, and when I felt myself swept shoreward and lifeward again. I know there are some who will say that the turning-point which I have called the moment of death was nothing more or less than the moment which marked the decline of the disease, and the return of vitality, but this theory, plausible and even probable as it seems, leaves the strangest part of my experience unexplained, and I cannot entertain it; neither, I think, will the reader, when he has heard me out.

Whether my death was succeeded by a season of slumber, in which certain divinely ordered dreams were caused to be dreamed by me, or whether God caused the hands on the dial of Time to be put back for a space in order that I might see the past as He sees it, I neither knew nor know; but I distinctly remember that the first thing of which I was conscious after my dissolution was that the events of my past life were rising before me. Yes, it was my past life, which I saw in that awful moment, my past life standing out in its own naked and intolerable horror, an abomination in the sight of God, and of my own conscience.

The hands on the dial of Time went back half a score, a score, and finally a score and a half of years, and once more I was a young man of twenty-one. The chambers in which I was then living were situated in one of the well-known Inns off Holborn, and the housekeeper of the wing where I was quartered was a widow, who, with her daughter Dorothy, a girl of seventeen, resided on the premises.

As it was Dorothy's part to wait upon the occupants of the chambers, she had occasion to come to my room several times in the day, and I could not help noticing her loveliness, which, indeed, reminded me not a little of my favourite Greuze picture. When I first knew her she seemed maidenly and modest, but was vain beyond a question,

and her manner to the opposite sex was shy
and self-conscious, with occasional dashes of
an artless and even childish coquetry which
was most bewitching. By this girl I was
irresistibly and fatally fascinated. I was
young, susceptible, and singularly impres-
sionable to female beauty, whilst the loneliness and the monotony of the life I was
leading were in themselves elements of
considerable danger; and to make matters
worse, it was only too evident that Dorothy
was not indifferent to my admiration. As I
knew that it was but the fascination of form
and feature which attracted me, and that
nothing but mischief was likely to come of
such a passion, I strove my hardest to steel
myself against her; but Fate seemed adverse,
for one summer evening while I was sitting
in my study, waiting for a friend, there burst
over London the most fearful thunderstorm

which I have ever witnessed. The lightning
was so vivid and the thunder so terrific, that
even I, who am by no means nervous about
such things, felt strangely moved and un-
settled; and I was not a little glad, therefore, to hear what I took to be my friend's
knock. When I went to the door, however,
I found that it was not he, but Dorothy, and
that she was white with fear, and trembling
from head to foot. "Oh, sir," she sobbed,
"mother's out, and there's no one else in but
you, and I'm so frightened that I can't stay
by myself. If you'll only let me be here till
she comes back, I'll be very quiet and not
disturb you in any way."

Knowing my weakness and her great
beauty, I had up to that moment studiously
refrained from allowing so much as a
wandering glance to rest on her; but I
could not avoid looking at her now, and I

remember that her eyes, bright and pitiful
and beseeching, " her bosom's gentle neigh-
bourhood," and the very consciousness of
her presence as she stood before me, set
my heart beating so wildly, that it was all
I could do to refrain from taking her in my
arms then and there, and telling her (forgive
the profanation of a holy word) that I
"loved" her.

The virtuous determination to be on our
guard against some besetting sin or con-
stitutional failing comes to us generally, *not*
during the moment of temptation, when we
are most in need of such a moral reminder,
but *after* the event, and when the determination is too late; but on this occasion I
heard the inward monitor speak out a timely
warning, and that with no uncertain tongue.
By a great effort I nerved myself to my
accustomed control, and though I knew

Dorothy would think me churlish and cruel,
I told her coldly that she had better go
downstairs and wait the return of her
mother. The words had scarcely time to
pass my lips (I doubt, indeed, if she could
have heard them), before they were lost
in a terrific thunder-peal, following almost
instantaneously upon a blinding flash of
lightning. It had been better for both of
us, as I have often since thought, if that
flash had struck us dead as we stood there;
for, with one cry of passion and fear, and
calling me by my name—my Christian name
—in a tone that none could misinterpret,
Dorothy flung her arms around me, and the
next moment I found myself pressing her to
my heart with a fierce and almost savage
exultation, and telling her, amid a score of
burning kisses, that I loved her.

Almost immediately afterwards we heard

the opening of doors, which indicated her
mother's home-coming, but not before
Dorothy had time to tell me in return that
she too loved me, and had always done so.
And then she slipped from my arms, and
tripped away with tumbled hair and flaming
cheeks to join her mother, turning as she
reached the door to look back with a shy
smile and to say—innocently and unsuspect-
ingly enough as I knew well—that the room
directly over mine was her own, and that
she often lay awake at night listening to my
restless pacing to and fro, and wondering
what could keep me up so late.

Of the hellish thought which rose in my
heart as I listened—the thought that she
would not refuse me admittance to her room
should I seek her there that night—she
could have had no suspicion, for it was a
thought of which, at any other time, I should

have deemed myself incapable. I remember
that I did not fling the hateful suggestion
from me, as I should have done an hour
earlier, although, passion-maddened as I was,
I recoiled from it, and vowed that I would
never entertain it. But I brooded over the
horrible idea, and sketched out how easily
it might be acted upon, were I the foul thing
to do it, which I still declared to myself I
was not. Had I arisen in trembling horror,
and thrust the vile conception from me, she
and I might even then have been saved, but
I let it enter and take up its abode in my
heart, and from thenceforward I strove to
drive it forth in vain.

Oh! in God's name, in the name of Love
and Truth and Purity, when any such evil
or impure thought so much as casts the
shadow of its approaching presence on your
soul, then, in all the strength of your man-

hood, arise and thrust it out, ere it be too late! Argue not, delay not, listen not, but hurl the loathsome whisper from you as though it were some poisonous reptile, and bid it be gone for ever!

From the moment that I gave audience to that messenger of Satan, hell and its furies laid hold on me. Sometimes I seemed to be gaining ground, sometimes I seemed to be recovering my balance of mind. "I *will* do the right!" I cried, "I will *not* be guilty of this accursed thing!" but even as I strove to fix my feeble purpose to the sticking point, some moral screw seemed to give way within me, and I felt that purpose ebbing away like life-blood from a fatal wound.

At last the struggle seemed to cease, and there was borne in upon me a sense of peace, deep, and sweet, and restful. I know now that it was but exhaustion consequent

upon the strain I had endured, that it was
nothing more than the inevitable re-action
from the high soul-tension to which I had
been subjected. To me, however, it seemed
as the very peace of God and as a sign from
heaven, and lulled into a false security, I let
my thoughts wander back to dwell again
upon the temptation. Need I tell the
remainder of my story? Need I say that
my passion had but simulated defeat, as
passion often does, in order that it might
turn in an unguarded moment, and rend me
with redoubled fury? The next moment I
saw my last gasping effort to will the right
sink amid the tempestuous sea of sinful
wishes, as a drowning man sinks after he
has risen for the third time; and deliberately
thrusting away, in the very doggedness
of despair, the invisible hand which yet
strove to stay me, I arose and sought

the room that I had prayed I might never enter.

\* \* \* \* \*

You may wonder, perhaps, how it is that I am able to recall so vividly the circumstances of an event which happened many years ago. You would cease so to wonder, had you seen, as I have seen, the ghost of your dead self rise up to cry for vengeance against you, and to condemn you before the judgment seat of God, and of your own conscience. For this was my first glimpse of Hell; this was my Day of Judgment. The recording angel of my own indestructible and now God-awakened memory showed me my past life as God saw it, and as it appeared when robbed of the loathsome disguises with which I had so long contrived to hide my own moral nakedness. "Sin looks much more terrible to those who look at it, than to those who do it," says the author of the "Story of an African Farm." "A convict, or a man who drinks, seems something so far off and horrible when we see him, but to himself he seems quite near to us, and like us. We wonder what kind of a creature he is, but he is just we ourselves." It was so indeed that I had thought and wondered. I had read often of "adulterers" and "murderers" in the newspapers, and had thought of them as I thought of lepers or of cannibals, in no way imagining that *my* youthful escapade could render such words applicable to me. I had accustomed myself to calling my crime "gallantry" in my own thoughts, and I should have regarded one who used harsher language as wanting in delicacy and in breeding; and now I found myself branded as "Murderer" and "Seducer" to all Eternity!

"Murderer!" you say. Yes, murderer, for seduction *is* moral murder; and the man who has thus sinned against a woman is fit only to stand side by side with him who has taken a life. Ay, and his is not seldom the more awful punishment, for God will as surely require the spiritual life at the hands of the seducer, as He will the bodily life at the hand of the murderer.

The one thing of all others which added to the unutterable horror of that moment, was the memory of the false and lying excuses with which I had striven to palliate my sin to myself. I remember that such excuses took form and shape, and haunted and tortured me like devils—as indeed they were—of my own begetting. "The relation of the sexes," I had often said when striving to silence an uneasy conscience, "Bah! it is but a yoke of man's imposing. I take the

F

woman I love to live with me, and she and
I are shunned as lepers.   Yonder is a man
who follows the same precedent and from
the same motive; and because a priest has
murmured a few words of sanction over the
contract, he and his partner are fêted and
flattered.   How can the indulgence of a
natural passion which in one set of circumstances is fair and honourable, in another
be sinful and foul?   Fair is fair, and foul
is foul, and no muttering of a man can
transform the one into the other."

This is the way in which I had repeatedly
striven to silence my conscience, and it is
but one instance of the way in which many
others on this earth are now striving to
silence theirs.   "For God's sake," I would
say to them, "beware!"   Such hardening
of the heart against the Holy Spirit, such
God-murdering (for it *is* the wish to kill

God, and to silence His voice for ever) is the
one unpardonable sin which is a thousandfold more awful in its consequences than is
the crime which it seeks to conceal. It was
the foulest stain on the soul of him who
hung by the dying Saviour, and it is, I
believe at this moment, the one and only
thing which still keeps Hell Hell, and Satan
Satan.

Must I write further of the torture-throes
of that awful moment, when I first saw my
sin in its true light? God only knows how
even now I shudder and shrink at the mere
thought of it; but I have told you of my
crime, and it is right that I should speak
also of my punishment. I remember that
when the realization of what I was, and
what I had done, was first borne in upon
me, I fell to the ground and writhed and
shrieked in agony. The tortures of a

material hell,—of a thousand material hells,
—I would have endured with joyfulness
could such torture have drowned for one
moment the thought-anguish that tore me.
Nay, mere physical suffering—physical suffering meted out to me as punishment,
and in which, though it were powerless
to expiate, I could at least participate by
enduring—I would have welcomed with
delirious gladness, but of such relief or
diversion of thought there was none. From
the mere mention of annihilation—the personal annihilation of soul and body, of
thought and sensation—I had ever shrunk
with abject loathing and dread; but to annihilation, had it been then within my reach,
I would have fought my way through a
thousand devils. But in hell there is no
escape through annihilation; suicide, the last

refuge of tyrannous and cowardly despair, is of none avail,

"And death once dead there's no more dying then,"

What had to be endured I found *must* be endured, and that unto the uttermost, for in all horrid hell there was no nook or cranny into which I could creep to hide myself from the hideous spectres of the past. I remember that I rose up in my despair, and stretching vain hands to the impotent heavens, shrieked out as only one can shriek who is torn by hell-torture and despair. I fell to the ground and writhed and foamed in convulsive and bloody agony. I dug my cruel nails deep into my burning eyeballs, and tearing those eyeballs from their tender sockets, flung them bleeding from me; but not thus could I blind myself to the sights

of hell, nor could mere physical pain wipe
out from my brain the picture of the ruin
I had wrought.

And then—but no, I am sick, I am ill,
I am fainting; I cannot, I cannot write
more.

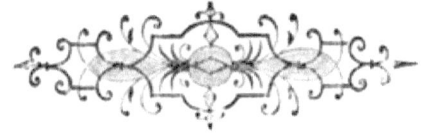

# CHAPTER VII.

"But there will come another era, when it shall be light, and when man shall awaken from his lofty dreams and find *his dreams still there, and that nothing is gone save his sleep.*"—JEAN PAUL.—*Preface to "Hesperus."*

THE following paragraph is taken from a diary which I kept before my decease. I will explain later on my reason for giving the extract here :—

"It has been said that no man can realize to the full the certainty of his own dissolution ; that each acknowledges the inevitability of death in regard to others and to the race, but cherishes a secret conviction that he himself will, through some strange and unforeseen circumstance, prove the solitary exception.

"Of the truth of this assertion as a general rule, I cannot of course speak, but I know that I at least have never so thought. On the contrary, there are moments when death (by which I do not mean annihilation, but the dying into life) seems the only certainty there is before me, all else being shadowy and unreal. I am a child of eternity dreaming the dream of time, and even while I dream I am half awake and know that I am but dreaming. Life is to me—not poetically only, but positively—a dream and unsubstantial. The world is a dream, things and persons are but dreams, and exist for me only in my thoughts of them. My self - consciousness becomes

awake, and I look in and down upon
myself with a wonder as fresh and novel
as if the mystery of my own existence
had never caused me wonder or surprise
before.　I stretch out my hand, as an
infant does, and open and shut the
fingers, and ask myself who I am and
what I am doing here.　I tell myself my
name, and I see that the hand, the body,
and the clothes that I look down upon
have a strangely familiar aspect, but the
name conveys no meaning to me, the
familiarity is but the familiarity of an oft-
dreamed dream, and is, I know, but the
sign that I am still dreaming.

" I look out each day upon the face of
the earth with as much wonder and surprise as if I were some new-comer there-
on, and were opening my eyes upon it for
the first and only time.　Upon London

and the life of it, though I passed half
my days within the sound of St. Paul's,
I gaze and wonder as upon some dream-
pageant, with ever-increasing awe. I look
up upon that ample dome, large-looming,
and brooding like a Presence athwart
the skies, until its surroundings and itself
and those who come and go in the streets
are to me as unsubstantial as 'a city
visioned in a dream.'

"So supremely conscious am I at such
times that

> 'We are such stuff
> As dreams are made of, and our little life
> Is rounded with a sleep,'

that were I, while this mood is on me,
to open my eyes one morning and find
that all this present world and its dream-
creations had passed away for ever, there
would hardly stir in my heart one

momentary thrill of surprise, for I should
but sigh and say, 'Ah, then, at last it
has come, and now I am asleep no
longer!'

"What the awakened life for which I
am waiting will be like, I know not con-
sciously, but something there is within
me that does know, and that has a dumb
inarticulate knowledge of it, like the
memory of a dream which we have not
all forgotten, yet cannot all recall. That
it will be *Life*, I am sure—a life which
though orbing in ampler cycle and vaster
sweep than this life, is yet on one and
the same plane with it, and in no way
separate and distinct. Nay, even now
this dream-world would seem to be sur-
rounded and insphered by the waking
one, even as 'time is but a parenthesis
in eternity;' for there are realities in

this unreal existence, flowers and faces,
love and poetry, and the morning and
evening skies, which have to me no part
in this perishable world, but which 'torment me ever with invitations to their
own inaccessible home.'"

I have transcribed this extract from
my earlier diary, not because I think
there is anything in it worth preserva-
tion, but because I believe it very aptly
illustrates the suitability of the punishment meted out to me in hell to my
own peculiar temperament. I was one of
those who lived only in thought. "The
world is a dream," I said, "things and
persons are but dreams, and exist for me
only in my thought of them." Hence to
make my punishment a *thought*, to con-
front me with the memory of my crime
and of its consequences, and to leave me

thus hell - haunted by the cry of an awakened conscience, was to inflict a torment upon me a thousandfold more terrible than material pain.

To those, however, who think with Heine, that "mental torture is more easily to be endured than physical pain," I have a word to say. When I was in hell, I saw there the souls of men and women whom I had known in life, and I learnt something of the nature of their sufferings. Unlike my own, that punishment was, in many cases, not mental but physical; and to those who are incapable of realizing what agony a thought can bring, let me say that hell has too its bodily punishment, and punishment from which there is no escape.

# CHAPTER VIII.

## *MAKE AN UNEXPECTED DISCOVERY IN HELL, AND MEET WITH AN OLD ACQUAINTANCE.*

"The servants said unto Him, Wilt Thou then that we go and gather them up? But He said, Nay; lest while ye gather up the tares, ye root up also the wheat with them. *Let both grow together until the harvest.*"— MATT. xiii. 28, 29, 30.

I COME now to what I think is the strangest part of my story. "When any one dies," I had been told in childhood, " he goes to one or the other of two places —either to hell or to heaven—according to whether he has been a good or bad man," and I recollect being not a little troubled in my childish mind as to what became of the people whose virtues were about equally matched with their vices (as I had even then discovered was not seldom the case), and whose chances between hell and heaven were what we used to call in my schoolboy days (I do not say it irreverently) a "toss-up."

"Even God must be puzzled sometimes," I used to think to myself, "to know what to do with the folk who are not wicked enough for hell, but a little too bad for heaven." Once after I had been taken to hear a long evangelical sermon, I thought I saw a way out of the difficulty by assuming that when God "weighed" a man (I use the phraseology of the sermon referred to, and I remember that not being clear as to how much of the language was figurative or otherwise I had an idea that souls really were weighed

in some sort of celestial balance) and found
him " wanting," He turned the scale in the
sinner's favour by pouring in some of the
blood of Christ. I can recall, too, that for
a day or two I went about fancying myself
quite a juvenile theologian, until the conviction that even God must draw the line somewhere, set me thinking that a good many
folk would thus be consigned to the bad
place for doing that which was only a very
little more wicked than was done by those
who were admitted to the good one.

My ideas about hell and heaven, even at
the time of my death, were not very clear and
not very many, although I do not think they
were more cloudy and less practical than are
the ideas entertained upon the subject by
other folk. I had been brought up in all
the old-fashioned orthodox and scriptural
notions, and "going to heaven" was as in-

separable in my mind from upward motion of some sort as "going to hell" was with downward motion. Each of the places was a separate and distinct one—the former being situated, according to my belief, somewhere in the direction of the zenith, while the latter I localized in the bowels of the earth, and connected in my thoughts with fire and darkness. Now let me give the results of my experiences, premising only that in regard to what I have to say about the after life, it must be understood that I am speaking only of that ante-chamber of the spirit-world—that in some sense purgatory, as I am half inclined to hold it—into which I have had admittance.

My experiences, then, are briefly these. *The good and the bad are not parted, but exist together as they exist here, and heaven and hell as separate places have no existence.*

G

I will tell you how I first came to discover
this. I have said that after my change (in
the spirit-world that which we call "death"
is spoken of as the "change") I awoke to
find myself in "hell," and I ought perhaps
to add that I used the word as indicating a
state of mental or physical suffering—in my
case the former—and not with any local
significance.

Even in hell, however, there are moments
when the intensity of the suffering is, for a
narrow space of time at least, relaxed, and
when the anguish-stricken spirit is mercifully
allowed a temporary reprieve. Such a moment occurred after the first awful paroxysm of
self-loathing and torture which I experienced
when my past life was made known to me in
its true colours, and it was in this saner, and
comparatively painless interval, that I met in
the spirit realm one whom I had known and

honoured on earth as a woman of the purest life and character. Being still under the impression that I was in " hell " in the sense in which I had been accustomed to think of that place, I started back upon seeing her, and hardly noticing her words of greeting, cried out in astonishment, " You here ! *You!* and in Hades ! "

" Where else should I be except where *he* is ? " she answered quietly, adding, as she observed my look of evident perplexity, " It is Arthur, of course, of whom I speak."

I remembered then that when I had known her first, her only living relative was a worthless brother of that name, to whom she was passionately attached, but who had been dead so long that I had hardly any recollection of him. Before I could question her further, I suppose she saw something in my face which told her all that was necessary to be known of my own story, for she suddenly burst into tears, and taking both my hands in her own with a gesture of compassionate grief, exclaimed, " Forgive me my foolish and selfish forgetfulness! Oh, I am so, so sorry!"

It was from her that I first gathered that even for me there was yet hope, and it was from her lips that I learned much of that which I have to tell of the spirit-world.

" Do you think," said she to me, when I had again expressed my wonder at finding that heaven and hell were not as I had supposed, separate places, " Do you think that I could be happy anywhere separated from my brother? Why, even Dives in the parable was unable to forget the five brethren he had left behind him, and cried out amid the flames, asking that Lazarus might be sent to warn them, lest they too should come to that place of torment. Is it likely, then, that any wife, mother, or sister, worthy the name, would be content to settle down idle-handed in heaven knowing that a loved one was in hell and in agony? I know there are folk on earth who try to smooth out the creases that crop up in the creed-roll of their convictions, by asserting that the truly re-generate soul will unconditionally surrender everything to the will of God, and that they, for their part, are quite prepared to leave the fate of their erring fellow-creatures in the hands of the Creator. I don't say that they are not right in so speaking, although, as far as I am concerned, I have more sympathy with old Dives and his wish to warn his sinning brethren. But how are we to know what is the final will of God in regard to one's fellows? When we are satisfied that a man who has fallen into the water is dead,

we may not unnaturally conclude that the
will of God, as far as this world is concerned,
is that he should come to an end by drowning, and we must bow to that will; but as
long as we can see a 'kick' left in him, we
feel that we must do all we can to bring him
round again.   Isn't that natural?"

I suppose I must have manifested some
surprise at the plainness of her speaking,
for after glancing at me for a moment with
an amused smile, and with a twinkle of her
old humour (I mean that kindly eye-twink-
ling of humour which is not far removed
from the trickle of a tear-drop, and which,
for all her piety, had been a noticeable
element in her personality), she said, as if
in reply to what was in my mind, "No, I
don't speak like a sanctified spirit, do I?"

I was a little taken aback by her question,
but answered that I was somewhat surprised

at the homeliness of her speech, but was glad to find that death had left her old personality unaltered.

"Of course it has," she answered, "my personality is just the old personality of my earth-life, and I should not wish it to be otherwise. To awaken after the change, which you call death, only to find that one's personality had been transformed into that of another person—no matter how excellent that other person might be—would not be immortality but transmutation. But you were about to ask me a question concerning my brother before we got upon the subject of personality," she continued; "you didn't put your question into words, but your looks expressed it, and thoughts cannot be concealed in the spirit-world."

"Yes," I said, "I had a question to ask

you, and it is this : You know how surprised
I was to find that heaven and hell are not,
as I supposed, separate places. Now what
is God's reason for allowing the good and
the bad to exist together here, as they do
on earth ? Is it because He shrinks from
breaking up the old family-life (as it must
be broken, if right-doers and wrong-doers
be set apart), and because He would still
use the influence of the good to reclaim the
evil ? "

"Even that," she said, "I cannot tell
you, for I am a mere child in His kingdom.
I do know that many of heaven's noblest
are engaged, as I am, in striving to stir up
souls to repentance ; but whether our efforts
to save the sinner from his sin after death
are of any avail, I cannot say positively, for
it has not been given me to know. We
are told that after His death our crucified

Lord preached to the spirits in prison;
and although the theologians will explain
it all away for you if you will let them, I
believe that He came here to hell in search
of the so-called lost, and I don't think I
can be doing anything opposed to His will,
in trying all I can to save my brother."

"When you and I were on earth together," she continued, after a pause, "you
once sent me a copy of the *Contemporary
Review*, containing an article written by
Dr. Knighton. The name of the article
was 'Conversations with Carlyle,' and the
writer related one conversation in which I
was very much interested, and which I have
often thought of since. I read it so many
times, that I think I can remember it word
for word.

"'I was going to tell you about an Indian
poem which some one sent me translated,'

said Carlyle. 'I think it was called the
"Mahabarat." It describes seven sons as
going off to seek their fortunes. They all
go different ways, and six of them land in
hell after many adventures. The seventh
is of nobler seed; he perseveres, fights his
way manfully through great trials. His
faithful dog, an ugly little monster, but very
faithful, dies at last. He, himself, fainting,
and well-nigh despairing, meets an old man,
Indra disguised, who offers to open for
him the gates of heaven. "But where are
my brothers?" he asks; "are they there?"
"No, they are all in hell." "Then I will
go to hell too, and stop with them, unless
you get them out." So saying, he turns off
and trudges away. Indra pities him, and
gets his brothers out of hell. The six enter
heaven first, the seventh stops. "My poor
faithful dog," says he; " I will not leave him."

Indra remonstrates, but it is useless. The faithful dog, ugly as he was, is too well remembered, and he will not have paradise without it. He succeeds finally, Indra relents, and lets even the dog in. But, sir,' added Carlyle, 'there is more pathos about that dog than in a thousand of our modern novels, pathos enough to make a man sit down and cry almost.'"

"Yes," I said, "I remember the story well. I wonder what old Carlyle would say about it now? Have you ever seen him here? or Emerson? or Richter? or Robertson of Brighton?"

"Robertson!" she answered; "as yet I know only one of the many circles into which the spirit-world seems naturally to resolve it; but I suspect that if you and I could see where Robertson is, we should find him infinitely nearer to the Father-heart

of the universe than I at least can for countless ages ever hope to attain !"

"What do you mean by 'circles'?" I said.
" Am I to understand that there is a kind
of sifting and sorting process going on, by
which each human soul is, on its arrival
here, assigned a fitting place and level
among his or her spiritual fellows ?"

" I don't know that I should express it
quite in those words," she answered, " although I cannot think just now of a less
clumsy way of putting it, but there is some
such gathering of like to like as that of
which you speak. The majority begin, as
we did, in this lower circle, and remain here
until they are fitted to move onward to a
higher sphere. Others take a place in that
higher sphere immediately, and some few
are led into the Holy Presence straightway.
To die is not to close the eyes on earth

merely to open them the next minute in
heaven ; it is not a sudden transition from
darkness to light, or from light to darkness.
No, it is a slow and gradual awakening, for
no human soul could bear so sudden a
shock. Your own transition was, comparatively speaking, an exceptionally rapid one,
but I know of some who have been 'changed'
for a quarter of a century, and are only
now becoming conscious of the fact. Of one
thing you may be certain, and that is that
God is never in a hurry in the education
of a human soul. He works in this world
as in the natural one, not by fits and starts
and sudden convulsions, but by slow and
imperceptible developments, and none but
Himself knows what He is going to make
of us before He has done—if indeed He
ever will have done, which I question.
Whatever sphere of work He may assign

to us here is the one for which He has
all along been preparing us. Our Saviour
told the disciples that in His Father's house
were many mansions, not one big one where
they were all to dwell together, but 'many
mansions,' and that He went to prepare
a place for them; and you may be positive
that He would not so have spoken were not
some individual preparation necessary.

"I do not know in which of these 'mansions of the blest' Frederick Robertson, of
whom you ask, is now dwelling, but you
must not think because his spiritual circle
is far removed from mine that all communication and companionship are cut off between
us. On the contrary, he is often, very often,
here, and I have not seldom held soul-com-
munion with him and felt his spirit near to
me. This circle, however, is but the outer
edge of the spirit-world — only one step,

indeed, removed from the life of the earth
and of the body—and I don't think we are
capable yet of understanding the finer dis-
tinctions of spiritual companionship." And
then her voice seemed to sound to me like
the voice of one in the far distance, I felt
the darkness closing in upon me on every
side, and knew that my hour of punishment
was again at hand.

Upon the details of that punishment it
would serve no good purpose again to dwell,
and if in the next two or three chapters I
make only a passing allusion to my subsequent sufferings in Hades, the reader must
understand that it is not because those
sufferings had in any way ceased to be, but
because I wish to put more prominently forward the singular facts in regard to the
condition of others, which came to my
knowledge during the time of my sojourning

in the spirit-world. That these facts were not without their own influence in bringing about the change in myself, hereafter to be described, will, I think, be apparent to all, but that change I shall not attempt to trace out, step by step, to its ultimate development. It is of what I saw and heard, rather than of what I endured, that I now come to speak, and although my recollections are all too disconnected and fragmentary I give those recollections just as they still linger in my memory, and without attempting to follow too closely the narrative of my own personal doings in Hades.

# CHAPTER IX.

### *I SEE SOME STRANGE SIGHTS IN HELL, AND AM FAVOURED WITH SOMETHING IN THE NATURE OF A SERMON.*

> "They eat, and drink, and scheme, and plod,
>  They go to church on Sunday;
> And many are afraid of God,
>  And more of Mrs. Grundy."

IT is a long time ago since Religion first took to preaching at the World, and now at last the World has grown wearied of it, and has taken in her turn to preaching at Religion; and in this verse by Mr. Locker-Lampson she has a text which is sternly, trenchantly, grimly true in its satire.

I know there are folk who affect to be scandalized at what they consider an irreverence, but I for one can recall no sermon in which the worldliness and the worthlessness of many so-called Christians have received as terrible a rebuke as they have in these lines by a writer of *vers de société*.

I will tell you why I have introduced this topic into my diary. When I was in hell, I saw one there whom, save for his averted looks and pitiable endeavours to escape my observation, I should probably have passed unnoticed. He was one of those at whom the verse I have quoted is directed. His pitfall in life had been nothing more vicious than vanity. He was a coward who was so blind in his cowardice that he feared God less than he feared Mrs. Grundy, and who, in order to secure the approval of man, had not scrupled to do that which he knew was hateful to his Maker. His life had been a living lie. Love of approbation was so strong in him that he was never happy except in perpetually posing and in endeavouring to pass himself off for that which he knew he was not. And with what result? That he had spent his days in preparing for himself his punishment. The one and only aim of his existence had been to win the approval of others, and, lo! one morning he awoke in Hades to find himself the despised of the despised and the laughing stock of the very Devil. He had so pandered to his love of approbation that it had grown at last into a disease, and I saw few more pitiable sights in my wanderings than that of this wretched creature, slinking shamefacedly through hell, and wincing, as from a blow, at the glance of every passer.

Of all vices none is so vindictive to its

wretched victim as vanity. It is continually craving for the wherewithal to gratify its insatiate appetite, whilst growing but the hungrier for a meal. The very clamorousness of its demands not seldom defeats its own purpose, for sooner or later it is sure to be discovered, and none of us honour the man whom we suspect of "jumping" to gain our good opinion. Of the power which vanity may acquire over a human soul I read lately an awful instance. We are told that the last emotion visible on the face of Pranzini, the French murderer, as he stood waiting to be despatched into eternity, was a simper of gratified vanity (and what share vanity had in bringing him to that scaffold only He who reads all hearts can tell) at being the prominent object of interest to so large and distinguished an assembly. And that as he was about to step with blood

upon his soul into the presence of the Great
Avenger !

\*     \*     \*     \*     \*

" Men create their God after their own
image," says Mr. Stigand in his " Life of
Heine "; " and it is a fact that the conception of God changes with the manners and
morals of a people. To our Puritan fore-
fathers He was a just but awful Judge, who,
from His home in the vast abysses of space,
kept an unwinking watch upon us, His
creatures, and, with eyes of telescopic
minuteness, noted every breach of His com-
mandments, in order that He might visit it
with a fiery and fearful vengeance. That
man-created God is no more : He is dead,
and another God reigns in His stead ; but in
our natural reaction from the conception of
the vindictive God of past generations, we
have come, in these days, to lose sight of the

fact that our God is a chastening one. Not only have we turned a deaf ear to the thunders and the threats of old-fashioned orthodoxy, with its talk of everlasting punishment and lakes of brimstone, but many of us *pooh-pooh* the thought of a hell at all, and speak of God as though He were a good-natured and weakly-indulgent parent, on whose leniency we might lightly presume, forgetting that sin—unrepented sin—never can and never must go unpunished.

It was in this contemptuously indifferent way that one whom I knew well on earth was accustomed to speak. He was a man of free and open disposition, with a perfect genius for friendship, but his life would not bear too close an inquiry. I remember his being warned in my presence of the punishment which must await the course he was pursuing, and his answering, as I had often heard him answer before, that even if he *were* on the road to hell (if, indeed, such a place existed, which he was inclined to doubt), he had at least the consolation of knowing that plenty of other "good fellows" were bound for the same destination, and that he was quite sure that he should feel more at home among the sinners in hell than he should among the saints in heaven.

Well, when I was in hell, I saw a sight there which is worth recording as an example of the ingenuity of the Devil in apportioning to each person the punishment best fitted to his individual case. I say "of the Devil," because I learned that he has a part (under certain restrictions and by Divine permission) in the imposition of necessary chastisement, and he is therefore an unwitting worker in the kingdom of heaven. He has indeed been such a worker from the

beginning, for in spite of his serpent-like
cunning and subtlety, he was the first fool,
and will be the last. The acknowledged
and ancient enemy of God, he is and has
been playing into the hands of the Almighty
for ages, and among all fools none is so
simple a fool as he.

The sight, then, to which I have referred
was that of a desolate plain, low-lying and
unlighted, and in the centre of it there
roamed one who called out ever and anon,
as if in search of a companion, but to whom
there came no answer save the distant echo
of his own cry. A more lonely and lifeless
spot I have never seen. The silence which
brooded over the place seemed sometimes to
oppress the forsaken wanderer like a presence, for, with a half-affrighted and despairing cry, he set off at a panic-stricken run, as
if seeking to escape this silence by flight;

but, notwithstanding his haste, he made, I
observed, no progress, for he was but moving
round and round in one continuous ring.   Of
this, however, he seemed unaware ; for once,
when he passed near me, I heard him cry
out as if in despair, " Is there no living soul
in all this void and voiceless desert ? "   And,
as he hurried by, and I caught a sight of his
face, I saw that it was the face of the man
who had said that hell would not be hell to
him so long as he and his boon companions
were together.

*       *       *       *       *

Another former acquaintance that I met
there interested me even more.   He was a
man whom I had always regarded as deeply
religious, and his presence in hell (by which
I mean as one who was undergoing punishment) was to me the greater cause for
surprise.

"What is it," I said to him, "that brings
you here? not impurity, surely? and I cannot think of any other reason."

"No," he answered, "it is not impurity,
for that was never one of my failings.  To
this day, I am unable to understand the
relish with which most young men (and
occasionally, be it said with shame, those
who are not young) listen to the kind of
conversation which is current sometimes in
the smoking-room.  We hold our handker-
chiefs to our noses when we pass a place
where there is an unpleasant odour, and turn
hastily away if we come upon a repulsive
sight; and impure talk affects me always as
does a disgusting object or a nauseous smell.

"You are surprised at finding me here in
hell, because you have always believed me
to be one who thought much and felt deeply
on religious subjects.  But you forget that

to have religious feeling, and to act upon
religious principle, are in many ways distinct. There are men who, though they are
naturally incapable of lofty thought, would
scorn to do anything immoral or mean; and,
on the other hand, there are men who feel
intensely on all religious subjects, who pray
fervently and often, sing hymns with eyes
streaming with tears of heartfelt earnestness,
and yet their actions are not seldom un-
worthy, and their lives will not bear too
close an inquiry. 'There is no self-delusion
more fatal,' as Mr. Lowell has said, 'than
that which makes the conscience dreamy
with the anodyne of lofty sentiment, while
the life is grovelling and sensual.' It is a
delusion which bids a man close his eyes
lest he see where he is going; it comes to
him with its harlot-beauties daintily draped
in the robes of an angel of light, and sings

hymns before the very gates of hell. It is because I am one who so deluded, or who tried so to delude himself, that you and I meet here to-day. We set out together with the broad path and the narrow path before us. You, by one fatal and irrevocable step, swerved to the broad path from the narrow, and that single step plunged you headlong and hopeless into this abyss. And I, well, I appeared to myself and to others to be walking in the narrow way; and yet, by the making of continual divergences, so trifling as to seem of but little or no account, I find myself eventually in the same awful abyss that you are in, and on a level fully as loathsome as your own. Though I have committed no such crime as you have committed, I was, in the petty details of my daily life, habitually untrue; and so the time came at last, in which, with every desire to serve

God faithfully and to follow the dictates of conscience, I found that the power to make my will subservient to my wishes had slipped unnoticed from me. Habit has the strength of a giant, for good as well as for evil, and the will to do right on every occasion is as much a matter of training as is mere physical strength. The man who is habitually untrue in small things, cannot, even though he wish it, do right in great ones, any more than the man of untrained muscle can, by a mere exercise of volition, lift weights which would try the practised athlete. The only way in which to become Christlike is not to endeavour to feel so, not to seek to arouse sentiment or emotion (as drunkards fly for strength to stimulants), but to make Christ-liness the persistent and unconditional *habit* of our lives. We must learn day by day to resist the first rising of a desire to do, or

to say, or to think, that which we know
diverges by the hundredth part of an inch
from the path which conscience would have
us to walk; and we must so school ourselves
that we can, by sheer force of will, rise
above the mood of the moment, so that we
act not by impulse or by inclination, but by
conscience."

He stopped, and, reading my thoughts,
said, in reply to them : "Yes, there is,
indeed, something grimly humorous in my
setting up to preach to others; but it cost
me my hope of heaven, and a lifetime, to
learn the lesson, and God knows I have
it by heart at last! One more illustration
and I have done. Let us suppose that you
and I are standing on the deck of a ship
which is steering straight for a certain haven,
and that you put your hand on the helm and
shift her a fraction of an inch from the line

on which she is running. The angle at which you have swerved from that line may be so utterly infinitesimal that it might be measured by a hair's breadth, but let that angle be carried out to its ultimate destination, and you will be borne miles and miles away from the harbour for which you are bound.

"Remember, then, when next you are called upon to make choice, be it in never so trifling a matter, between good and evil, between obeying conscience or disobeying her, that you are choosing in that moment between hell and between heaven, not for to-day, this week, or to-morrow, but for eternity!"

# CHAPTER X.

## A LOVE STORY IN HELL.

"And shall my sense pierce love,—the last relay
  And ultimate outpost of eternity?"—D. G. ROSSETTI.

SOME years ago, a near relative of mine, the editor of a certain paper, was taken seriously ill, and was told by the doctors that complete rest was absolutely necessary for his recovery. As I had frequently assisted him in the preparation of "copy," and was acquainted with the routine of his office, it was arranged that I should attend on certain days in each week, and be answerable for the work during his absence.

The journal was one which was made up largely of extracts from other papers, and my duties consisted less in the selection of original matter, than in the more prosaic plying of paste-brush and scissors ; but the number of manuscripts received was large, and for a week or two at least I tried conscientiously to give each separate packet something like a fair consideration. I remember that the very first manuscript on which I was called to pronounce judgment was one entitled, " The Strange Confessions of a Bachelor." It is too lengthy to be printed here in full, but as the love-story from which my chapter takes its heading was largely attributable to the publication of this manuscript, I have transcribed some paragraphs from it, which I think will serve to give the reader a general idea of its tone.

THE STRANGE CONFESSIONS OF A BACHELOR.

"Yes, I am in love, although as yet I
could not tell what the name of my love
is or will be. But in every inspired poem
or perfect picture, in the soaring and sobbing of music, in sunrise and sunset, or in
the sighing of the wind upon my cheek,
there is something which speaks to me of
her, and which beckons my spirit forth in
search of her, as if by the leading of an
unseen hand. And sometimes, but only in
my dreaming, musing moments, my thoughts,
as they wander forth into the blue expanse
around me, take colour and shape, and I
see her standing by a tiny cot in a cosy
room where the warm firelight flickers on
walls gay with pictures. I see her bend
with eyes that brim with tears of blessing
to fold two dimpled hands together, and to

listen to a baby voice which whispers after
hers the hallowed words to 'Our Father in
Heaven.' And as the little voice dies away
into the holy hush of the last Amen, and
the little lids droop like the petals of a primrose over the tired eyes, my dream-picture
changes again, and I am rambling among
the walks I love so well, but no longer
alone, no longer wrapt in melancholy musing, for—now trudging cheerily along with
hand clasped fast in mine and face upturned
to listen, now darting bird - like aside in
search of fly or flower—there journeys ever
with me my little son and hers. We wander merrily through that sunny stretch of
meadow—the children's meadow, as we call
it—where the grass grows lush and long,
and where the blithe day through the sky-
lark ever sings and soars ; we cross the stile
and enter the shady shelter of the 'Lover's

Lane,' dark, as it always is, with the dense green of overarching ash and hazel, and then we reach that sunny, wind-swept and sloping hillside, where he and I love to linger, watching the slow sailing of stately clouds above, or listening to the tinkle and purl of the brooklet which ripples over the pebbles in the valley far below. In the joyous wonder of the child heart beside me at all that is beautiful in this beautiful world, I forget the books and the making of books with which my brain is busied; and when the first flush of rapture is over and the little brain has sobered into calm, I tell my boy of the Brother-Lord who loves him, and who was once such a little child as he, and of the dear Lord-Father by whom all that is beautiful was made."

The writer of the "Confessions" then goes on to speak of love, and of the woman he loves; but as his concluding paragraph will sufficiently serve to give an idea of his thoughts on the subject, it is hardly necessary to quote the passage in full. "Yes, I love her, I love her truly, and she too loves me, or will. It is not blind love, or foolish idolatry. She knows all my faults —the pitiful paltriness of my life, the selfish acts and foolish words, the vanity and thè vice—she knows them all, and yet she loves me, me, not them, but the true me which these faults cannot altogether conceal from her, for she knows that they are not my life, but the trouble of it. So also is my love for her. I love her not only for her present self, but for the sake of the self she is seeking to be—the self which in some measure indeed she now is; for that which in our truer moments we have striven to be; the Ideal upon which our eyes are ever fixed,

to which (no matter how sorely we may
have sinned against it in the struggle of the
day) our thoughts return at night with but
the more unutterable if despairing longing
and love—*that* in some manner we are, and
shall be, notwithstanding our ever-recurrent
failure and sin.

" I do not ask or expect that she shall be
always true to her high ideal, for I know
that to none of us is it given to walk with
unfaltering feet. I remember, too, that she
is no angel, but a woman with womanly
weakness and human faults, for all of which
I am touched with true and tender sympathy, to love her not the less, but the more.
But that she should *have* such an ideal, and
be capable of such an aim—for that reason,
if for no other, I must love and honour her
with the deepest love and honour of my
soul. I am not so blind as to suppose it

will be all summer and sunshine in the life
which she and I will, I hope, one day lead
together. I know my own evil nature too
well not to be aware that there will be times
when she will find it hard to prevent love
being turned into loathing and confidence
into contempt; and I think, with sinking of
spirit, of the sore disappointment she will
feel when she finds what a shabby-souled
common-place creature her husband is, compared with the being into whom her love
had idealized him. At such times of de-
spondency, however, I try to remember what
Miss Muloch has said about wedded life—
and who has written more helpful words
than she? 'I would have every woman
marry,' she says, 'not merely liking a man
well enough to accept him as a husband,
but loving him so wholly that, wedded or
not, she feels she is at heart his wife, and

none other's, to the end of her life. So
faithful that she can see all his little faults
(though she takes care no one else shall
see them), yet would as soon think of loving
him the less for these, as of ceasing to look
up to heaven because there are a few clouds
in the sky. So true and so fond that she
needs neither to vex him with her constancy
nor burden him with her love, since both
are self-existent and entirely independent of
anything he gives or takes away. Thus she
will marry neither from liking nor esteem,
nor gratitude for his love, but from the
fulness of her own. If they never marry,
as sometimes happens . . . God will
cause them to meet in the next existence.
They cannot be parted ; they belong to one
another.'

" These are helpful words, and true ; but
there is a passage by poor George Eliot

(alas for that adjective!), which to me is still more beautiful, and with which I cannot do better than conclude. 'What greater thing is there,' she says, 'for two human souls, than to feel that they are joined for life, to strengthen each other in all labour, to rest on each other in all sorrow, to minister to each other in all pain,' and, 'to be one with each other in silent, unspeakable memories at the moment of the last parting?'"

I was interested in this article as well as in the writer, and asked him for further contributions. He responded by sending a couple of sonnets, and although the "swing of his arm" was, to quote Rossetti, "freer in prose than in verse," I accepted, and printed them in the journal of which I had charge. When I came to know him afterwards, I found that he was young, and of that highly-strung nervous and poetic temperament which often proves little less than a calamity to its possessor. A more morbidly sensitive being I never met. The emotional part of his nature seemed in excess, and he felt all—the small as well as the great, the pleasant as well as the painful—intensely. His nervous vitality was too near the surface. He was easily "worked-up," and took life, or rather its incidents, too seriously. The one intellectual thing which men of such a temperament would be wise to refrain from doing, is not seldom the very thing they do—abandon themselves passionately to the pursuit of poetry. After that there is little hope for them. The world may be the richer by many a work of art, but from thenceforth and for ever Sorrow will have them for her own.

" Poetry strikes as nothing else does, deep into the roots of things," says Elizabeth Stuart Phelps, and " one finds everywhere some strain at the roots of one's heart." Moreover, the pursuit of poetry is a practice which as surely grows upon one as does the use of drug or opiate, and my advice to the men and women of a highly-strung and supersensitive temperament—if they wish to make comfort their first considera- tion—is, "Avoid poetry as you would poison, making instead a study of that which is animal and coarse. Music and all other ' softening' influences you will, in accordance with the contention of Plato in ' The Re- public,' deliberately eschew, striving rather to acquire that delightful pachydermatous condition of feeling and enviable indifference to the susceptibilities of others, which add so immeasurably to the comfort of life."

However, to return to the writer of " The Strange Confessions." The number of the journal containing his article had not been published more than a couple of days, before I received a letter signed by a lady who was unknown to me, asking that I would favour her with the address of the contributor. I replied, of course, that I could not do so without his permission, but that if she wished to be put into communication with him, and would send a letter addressed to the office of the paper, it should be duly forwarded. She did so, and when, as was natural enough, he wrote a cordial reply, she found something else in his letter about which to question him, and a correspondence consequently ensued. Whether she was or was not a heartless and accomplished flirt I never knew; but if ever a woman deliberately set herself to win, and—as subsequent

events showed—to break a man's heart, it
was this lady. I learned afterwards that
she was very beautiful, and as she herself
wrote occasional tales and verses for the
magazines, it was not to be wondered at
that my contributor should be greatly interested in her epistles. She succeeded before
long in making his acquaintance, and set
herself to carry on in earnest the work
which her insinuating letters had begun.
She did not, however, find him quite the
easy prey which she had perhaps expected;
for though it is certain that he loved her
from the moment of meeting, he was shy
and self-depreciatory, and sought persistently
to avoid her. But she paused at nothing
to effect her purpose. She had set her
heart upon "a scalp," and by looks, words,
and deeds, she strove to convince him that
she loved him, and strove at last success-

fully. I remember meeting him one morning, and thinking, as I watched the light
which came into his face when he spoke of
her, of the graceful lines in Mr. Austin
Dobson's " Story of Rosina." In the poem,
however, it is the woman, and not the man,
who is heart-broken :—

> " As for the girl, she turned to her new being,
>     Came, as a bird that hears its fellow call ;
>   Blessed as the blind that blesses God for seeing ;
>     Grew as a flower on which the sun-rays fall,
>   Loved if you will ; she never named it so ;
>     Love comes unseen, we only see it go."

When I saw him again all was over. I had
sought him out in his chambers, not having
heard from him for a month, and he did not
hear me enter. Her portrait (the one she
had given him) was before him, and he had
fallen by the table, half-kneeling, half-lying,
with his head on his arm. It is a fearful
thing to hear a strong man sob as he was

sobbing then! God grant that I may never
hear another, or see a face of such hopeless
haggard misery as was his when he raised
it!

It is not of him, however, that I wish now
to speak, but of her. Of all the faces which
I saw in hell, there was one which had for
me a fascination beyond any other. It was
the face of a beautiful woman, queenly of
manner and fair of figure as a full-blown lily,
and with those deep dark eyes that *seem*
to shine out from soul-depths, deep as the
distant heaven, and yet *may* mean no more
than does the shallow facing of quicksilver
behind a milliner's mirror. I recognised
her instantly by the portrait, and never out
of hell have I seen such misery on any
woman's face as I saw on hers. The sentence in punishment of her sin was a strange
one. It was that she should now love him

whose heart she had broken, with the same
passionately intense but hopeless love with
which he had loved her. It was a just but
awful retribution. As some death-stricken
and hunted creature presses frantically on
as if to escape the arrow that it carries in its
breast, so, heedless of all that was passing
around her, heedless of shadow or shine, she
pressed on and on through the realms of
hell, her eyes fixed and wide-distended in
agony, and her hands clutching ceaselessly
at her bosom, as if the heart of her were
being riven in twain. "O God!" I heard
her cry, as she passed me, "my heart is
broken! my heart is broken! and, alas, one
cannot die of a broken heart in hell."

I saw her once again. She had fallen to
the ground, and with hopeless hands pressed
against burning brows was writhing as if in
physical pain, and with her very soul con-

sumed of passion. One whom I knew—it was his sister—was kneeling beside her, and with gentle words besought her to calm herself, but she pushed the ministering hand away despairingly, crying out: "A heart cannot break as mine is breaking without a shriek. If I had loved him, and he me, and he had died," she said, "I could have borne it, knowing that I should meet him hereafter, but to live loveless through a loveless Eternity, *that* is the thought which kills me;" and then with a great cry of, "Oh! why should a merciful God let any of His creatures suffer as I am suffering now?" she rose up, and fled away before me.

I never saw her again, nor do I know whether or not it was given her to win back the love she had lost; but, after she had gone, I turned to his sister—the woman who

K

had striven to comfort her brother's betrayer
—saying that I thought the punishment
greater than the sin.

"Greater than the sin!" was the reply.
"It may be that, being his sister, I judge
her harshly; but if yours is the most awful
crime which your sex can commit against
womanhood, then it seems to me that hers—
a like breach of trust—is the blackest sin
which a woman can commit against a man.
Nor can it be said of hers that it was the
deed of a moment—a moment of over-
mastering passion, for it was deliberate and
cruel. I say that that woman killed my
brother!" she cried fiercely; "killed him
body and soul, and sent him away heart-
broken, and bereft of faith in womanhood
and in God. And to gratify what? her
vanity—a passion as selfish and hateful, if
less brutal, than your own. You have

recognised the loathsomeness of your act; but she, God help her! thinks of nothing but herself, and while she so thinks, heaven itself would be but hell to her, and in all hell there is as yet for her no hope of heaven."

# CHAPTER XI.

*THE MYSTERY OF "THE DEAD WHO DIE."*

"Of all these mysteries there is none which fills me with such abject horror and dread as the mystery of 'the dead who die.'"

"Through many days they toil ; then comes a day
They die not,—never having lived,—but cease ;
And round their narrow lips the mould falls close."

*Rossetti*—"The Choice."

IT may occur to those of my readers who have neglected to bear in mind the concluding words of Chapter VIII., that notwithstanding the remorse which I have pictured myself as suffering in Hades, I do not appear to have been altogether indifferent to the consolations of social intercourse, and that existence in the Unseen, as represented in the pages of this diary, would seem to consist largely of conversation between the "spirits in prison." But because I have confined myself in my last three chapters to the relation of such facts in regard to the condition of others, as, either through observation or conversation, came to my knowledge in the course of my singular experiences, it must not be supposed that my own sufferings had in any way ceased. What those sufferings were as described by me in my sixth chapter, they continued to be during the whole of the time in which it was ordained that I should remain in Hades, and each of the conversations here recorded took place during that comparatively painless interval of which I have elsewhere spoken, and was separated from the conversation preceding

or following it by a space of terrible pain.
With which necessary reminder I pass on
to tell of "the dead who die."

During the time of my wanderings in
the spirit world, it happened that I had
occasion to speak to one to whom I was
personally unknown, but who had lived for
many years in a country town in which I
had myself once resided. Though comparatively guiltless, as I learned he was,
of any criminal offence, he seemed to be
incessantly consumed by a spirit of strange
unrest, and I noticed that, even in his
moments of reprieve, he appeared unable
to free himself from some singularly dis-
turbing thought. I was aware that he had
at one time been intimate with a former
neighbour of mine, and something in our
conversation recalling this man's name to
my memory I asked my companion if he

knew " what had become of Henry
Marshall ? "

The words had scarcely fallen from my
lips before there passed over his features
a spasm of uncontrollable fear, and with a
quick gasping cry, and covering his . face
with his hand, as if to shut out some
ghastly vision, he exclaimed : " He is dead ;
he is dead—but why do you speak of him ?
Know you not that he is of the dead who
die ? "

" Of the dead who die ? " I repeated
wonderingly; " I do not understand you.
Surely all who are dead must die ? "

To this he made no answer, and seeing
that he was strangely moved, I forbore to
question him further, but by-and-by he
became calmer and of his own accord continued the conversation.

" You asked me about Henry Marshall,"

he said, "and I will tell you all I know about him ; but first let me explain that, next to the love of money which has been my ruin, my sorest hindrance on earth was my unbelief and faithlessness ; and that here in hell the punishment of the unbeliever is that he shall be consumed by the anguish of his own unbelief. Once when I *might* have believed, I would not, and now, though I would believe, I cannot, but am for ever torn by hideous apprehensions and doubts as to my own future and the future of those dear to me. Moreover, there are many things which, clear and plain as they may be to the faithful of heart and to the believing, are to my doubting eyes wrapt around in mystery and in gloom. Into these mysteries it has been ordained as part of my punishment that I shall ever desire to look, and of all these mysteries there is not one which fills me with such abject horror and dread as the mystery of the dead who die."

"Of the dead who die?" I said again; "what do you mean by those strange words?"

"They are my words," he cried excitedly, and with a hysterical laugh, "mine, mine; the words I use to myself when I think of the mystery which they strove so carefully to conceal from me, but which for all their cunning I have discovered. Listen, and I will tell you about it. When I first came here, I saw, either in hell or in heaven, the faces of most of the dead whom I had known on earth, but some faces there were (Henry Marshall's was one of them) which I missed, and which from that time to this I have never seen. 'Where, then, are they?' I asked myself, 'since

neither earth, hell, nor heaven knows them
more?   Has God some fearful fate in store
for the sinner, which may one day fall
upon me and mine, as it has already fallen
upon them?'   As I felt the shadow of that
dark misgiving resting on my heart, I knew
that for me another horror had arisen in
hell, and that rest thenceforth there could be
none until I had solved the mystery.

"And so it came about that all the
moments of my release from suffering were
spent in the search for those missing faces.
Sometimes I took counsel with those who
were in hell as I was, but they could
teach me only that which I already knew ;
sometimes I asked the help of the souls
in Paradise, but they told me nothing save
that I must be no more faithless but
believing.  ·And then I sought to know of
the angels where were those lost ones, but

with a look of sad and pitiful meaning, they passed on and left me unanswered. Ah! but they could not hide their secrets from me! No, no, I was not one of the credulous, nor was I to be put off with a frown, and I have found out their mystery, and you shall share it.

"When you and I were children, we were taught that every human being is made in the image of God, and is born with an immortal soul. But they did not tell us that just as neglected diseases can kill the body, so unchecked sin can kill the soul, and that we have it in our power to so deface the Divine Image that we become like unto, if not lower, than the beasts which perish, and die out at our deaths as they. But it is so, and that is what I meant when I said that he of whom you asked was 'of the dead who die.'

" You shake your head, and mutter that I
am mad, and that you cannot credit such a
statement. Well, perhaps I am mad—mad
with the horror of my unbelief; but why
should it not be as I say, I ask you? I
have brooded over it all a thousand times,
and am convinced that I have solved the
riddle, and I will tell you why I think so.

"God is answerable to Himself for His
actions, and when He made man, He made
a man, and not a puppet—a being of infinite possibilities for good as well as for
evil, and to whom it was given to choose for
himself between the doing of the right or
the wrong. But God knew that many of
those whom He so made would sin away
all memory of their Divine origin. God did
not *will* it so, for He made us men, not
machines, and the evil we do is of our own
choosing, but God *foreknew* it; and, fore-

knowing that, God owed it to Himself not to call a creature into being, the result of whose creation would be that creature's infinite and eternal misery. No, even the Omnipotent dared not perpetrate so wanton and wicked a deed as that, for God is the inexorable Judge who sits in judgment upon God; and hence it was that He decreed that those for whom there could be no hope of heaven should die out at their deaths like the brutes. Doesn't that seem to you a probable solution? and isn't it rational and feasible upon the face of it? Our life—such as it is—is from God, and may not God take His own again, and withdraw that life if He wish it? and could anything better happen to many people whom you and I know, than that they should be allowed to die out, and the very memory of them pass away for ever?"

I was convinced that he was mad—mad, as he had himself hinted, with the horror of his unbelief; but I was interested in what he had to say, and in his singular fancies.

" Tell me more of these missing faces, and of the ' dead who die,' " I answered.   " Who are they, for the most part ?—murderers and criminals of the most bestial nature ? "

" Not always," he replied excitedly, " not always; and that is the reason why I am so fearful about my own future.   Most of them are those who in their lifetime were regarded as belonging to the respectable classes, and who, so far from having come at any time within reach of the law, were looked upon as good citizens and estimable members of society.   Shall I tell you what killed the immortal soul in them, and in me, and turned us into mere animated clay, fit only to die out like the beasts which perish ?

It was money—money, the love of which is often more deadening to the spiritual nature than actual vice or sin.

"I set out in life with one steadfast purpose before me—the purpose of devoting myself body and soul to business and to the making of money. It was not that I was indifferent to the attractions of a profession, and still less that I was wanting in appreciation of higher things, for I liked books and pictures and music. Sometimes, too, when I was listening to my sister's singing of Herrick's lines, 'To Anthea,' or to Ben Jonson's 'Drink to me only with thine eyes,' I felt bitterly the littleness of my aims, and seemed to know, as I never knew at any other time, what it was to love a woman with that high, whole-hearted, and deathless devotion which brings redemption and ennoblement to the soul of the man to whom

it comes.   But I said to myself : ' Patience ;
first of all let me grow rich ; let me make
all the money I can get together, and then,
when I have sufficient for all my requirements, I will forsake the money-making, and
turn my thoughts to love and poetry and
pictures; and through them, perhaps on to
religion, for I knew even then that though
love and poetry are not religion, that they
yet serve, before a higher faith has been
called into being, to keep the life of the
soul alive, and to open up the way for
holier things.

And so I became what is called a good
business man.   I made business the motive
of my life.   I thought of nothing else, and
read nothing but the papers, and these I only
scanned for the purpose of observing the
influence of political or other passing events
upon the markets.   At last I became rich.

And with what result? That when I no
longer needed business, I found I could live
no longer without it; that it had become my
life, and I its slave, and that I could awaken
no lasting interest in anything which did
not pertain to the making of money. It is
true that I had at that time a wife and
children (the former of whom I had married
chiefly for her fortune), and was not without
a certain half-selfish love for them as part
and parcel of myself; that I possessed a
handsome house and gardens in which I took
pride as being of my own acquirement; and
that I went into society with enjoyment;
and found a certain pompous pleasure in
extending my patronage to Sunday-schools,
bazaars and Young Men's Christian Associa-
tions. But where my treasure was, there my
heart was also, and at heart I was a business
man, and nothing more. I did not know

L

myself then as I do now, and so far from
being in any way dissatisfied, I had no more
suspicion that I was other than one of the
most enviable of men, than has the grinning
savage with his handful of beads. But I
know now the thing I am, and what I have
missed, and I tell you that the most sorely
swindled simpleton in existence is the man
whose business capability is so keen, that
though he has never been bested in a bargain, he has bartered away his own happiness for a bauble, and (so skilful a schemer
to defraud us is old Satan) has become bankrupt of all that makes life worth the living,
in order that he may boast a heavy balance
at his banker's!

Yes, I was a good business man—a smart
and shrewd business man, as business men
go—and I know much of such men and of
their transactions; and I tell you that, since

the days of Judas Iscariot, the money-lover
and grubber who sold his God for thirty
pieces of silver, as thousands are selling their
infinite souls this day, there have been no
more soulless and selfish creatures upon
God's earth, than the men who have made
what should be a means to an end an end in
itself, and who live *for* business, instead of
*by* it.

They go to church, many of them, on
Sundays, and subscribe liberally to coal
clubs and soup kitchens, thinking, poor
fools! to offer such acts as those as a set-off
to God for the sordid self-seeking which has
been the secret of their success in their
commercial calling; never suspecting that in
their respectable selfishness and sordidness
of spirit, they are lower in the scale of being
and farther from the kingdom of heaven
than is the lurking prostitute shivering at the

street corner, or the drunken sot reeling home after a night's debauch.

That they must die out at their deaths, as do the beasts, I am convinced, for what can God find for such men to do in heaven?—men to whom the earth, its prototype, is nothing but a gigantic shop, and to whom Music, Art, and Song are but as dead letters and foolishness; men who are susceptible to no emotion save the greed for gain; and who have let the infinite soul within them pine away and perish for the want of the wherewithal to keep that soul alive.

"And I, I am one of them, and am of the dead who die! I have bartered away love and life and happiness for such Dead Sea fruit as this; I who once was young, and not altogether, as I now am, a soulless creature of clay! For I can remember the time when flowers, pictures, beautiful faces and music set stirring always some strong emotion within me, in which it seemed that I saw hidden away in a crystal cell in the depths of my own strange heart, the shining form of a white-robed Soul-maiden, who cried out to me, ' Ah ! cannot you make your life as pure and beautiful as the flowers and the music, that so you may set me free ? '

" But I chose the ignoble part, and gave myself up body and soul to the greed for gain. And often in the hour when, tempted by an evil thought, I turned to do some shameful or selfish action, I seemed to see the white arms of the Soul-maiden uplifted in piteous entreaty to heaven, until at last the time came when her voice was silent, and when I knew that I had thrust her down and down into a darkness whence she would never again come forth !

"And now nor picture, nor poem, nor music moves me more, for the soul of me is dead!—is dead! and I have become like unto the beasts that perish, and know not that at any moment I may flicker out like a spent taper, and become as the dead who die!"

So saying, he burst into a shriek of insane and unearthly laughter, and foaming at the mouth like a madman, turned from me, and fled gibbering into the night.

## CHAPTER XII.

### *I SEE THE BROTHER WHOM WE HAVE ALL LOST.*

"YOU believe probably in God, in Christ, and in Immortality, and you look with joy and gladness to the life beyond the grave. Probably, too, you have suffered, as we all have at some time, from bodily pain, mental affliction or bereavement, until your heart has been broken and crushed, and you have felt that you could bear your burden no longer were it not for the consolation that sorrow can last no longer than life, and that the next

world will set this world right. But have
you never asked yourself, ' How if it should
*not* be so after all ? How if I should open
my eyes in the next world to find again
all the old sorrows, the old heart-burnings,
and the thousand and one trivialities which
have made this world so weary, stale, flat,
and unprofitable ?' Have you never con-
sidered that the mere fact of the existence
of these sorrows in this world—the only
one of which you know anything—is in
itself a reason why it is likely that such
sorrows, or similar ones, should exist in the
world of which you know nothing ? And
have you never recognised that your failures
have been the life-element of your successes,
and that, since failure is the law of progress,
an existence in which all your endeavours
were successful would probably become
monotonous and tame ? "

The above is an extract from a letter
(it lies on the desk before me) from one
whom I had known in my early boyhood,
and who had been for many years my
constant companion and friend. Had she
continued to be my companion it is possible
that my story might have been a different
one, but she went to live in America some
months before I was twenty, and I never
saw her again until the day that she and
I stood face to face in the spirit-world—I
in hell and she in heaven.

After we had exchanged greetings, and
each had told the other what was necessary
to be known of the past, the conversation
turned upon the subjects which we had so
often discussed in our letters. " Tell me,"
I said, "now that you really find yourself
in heaven, if you are in every way peacefully and perfectly happy."

"One moment, before I give you an answer," she replied. "You are not altogether wrong in calling this heaven, although it is little more than the antechamber between earth and heaven. It is my heaven at present, but it will not be my heaven always, any more than it will be always your hell, and although it is heaven, it is not *the* heaven. Of that neither you nor I can form any shadowy conception. Now for your question. There is only one thing which troubles me, and that is ignorance. I had always thought that in the spirit-world one would know everything. I don't mean that I expected to find myself omniscient, but I did think that I should know all one would wish to know. I need hardly tell you I was wrong. With whatever knowledge we have acquired and with whatever intellectual ability we have developed up to the point of our leaving the earth-world, with that, and with no more, do we make our first start in the spirit realm. I do think our capability of intuitionally apprehending truth is in some way intensified by the transition which you speak of as death : but of intellectual change there is absolutely none ; and there are things relating to the after-life, as well as to the earthly one, concerning which (never having studied them whilst I was in the body) I am far more ignorant than are many dwellers under the sun."

"That I can well believe," I replied ; "but putting aside the fact that you are troubled sometimes by a consciousness of ignorance, tell me if in other respects you are happy."

"No good can come to one of being in a place where everything is too easy," she

answered, "and if heaven were the abode
of perfect happiness—this heaven, I mean—
I think we should find it somewhat weari-
some. When I was on earth I longed for
heaven, *not that I might be delivered from
sorrow, but from sinfulness;* and I think
I may say that I am as happy here as my
failures will let me be."

"Your failures!" I exclaimed, wonderingly, "your failures!"

"Yes," she said, "my failures. On earth
failure is, as you know, the law of progress,
and even here progress is only achieved
through that which is, after all, in some
degree a non-success. I don't quite know
how to make my meaning clear to you,
but perhaps we can't do better than look
back to the old earth-life for an illustration.
That earth-life—the life which we lead on
earth, I mean—is, as you know, poor, pitiable

and paltry; we feel it so, we cannot but
feel it so, when it is viewed in the lofty
light of our possibilities. Each morning
finds us beginning the world afresh, and
with the high hope that at last the time
has come when we shall be true to ourselves and to our aspirations, that at last
we shall veritably and indeed do some
lasting work for God and for our fellow-
creatures. And each evening! ah! each
evening! is it not ever the same sad story,
ever the same old bitter experience? You
have spoken of it yourself in those verses
you sent me so many years ago:

> " 'Each morning hails a new Endeavour's birth,
>   Each evening weeps its pitiful corpse before.'

" Hardly has the freshness faded out of
the morning air before the world spirit is
at our side again; she is whispering in

our ear; her white wooing arms are around
us; her warm breath is on our cheek; there
is a brief,—how brief and feeble!—attempt
at resistance, and then, ah! then, we are
broken and undone.    And often as, with
lips hot and dry, with cheeks fevered and
flushed, we look back to that serene-souled
self, which but a few short hours ago stood
in rapt adoration under the silence of a
midnight sky, and held high communion
with its Creator, we can hardly bring ourselves to believe that we and it are one
and the same being.    Yet, in spite of
the paltriness of the earth-life, in spite of
the vice, and the shame, there is one
element in the strife which lends dignity
even to our very failures, for in our battling
against the ever-present evil, and in our
struggle towards the ever-unattained good,
we come within sight of a possibility, higher,

perhaps, than that of which even angels can conceive. The *sin and the shame are after all but human; the effort and determination to overcome them are Divine.*

"Well, without some sense of difficulty to be overcome, some sense even of comparative failure, this effort and this determination could never be; and in heaven, the place of infinite progress and possibilities, there is a certain Divine discontent which I know not how to explain better to you than by calling it the heavenly counterpart of this earthly effort.

"But now tell me about yourself," she said, after a moment's pause, "for I can see that you have been through sore suffering since you came here."

Through sore suffering I had indeed been, and had already grown old in hell, but the lines which she had quoted from my boyish

verses, and the words she had said about
the "divine discontent" of heaven, had set
stirring some hidden spring in my memory,
and at the time she spoke I was thinking of
what Robert Louis Stevenson has said about
"that little beautiful brother whom we once
all had, and whom we have all lost and
mourned—the man we ought to have been,
the man we hoped to be." She must have
known what was in my thoughts, for, taking
my hand in her own, she repeated some
verses which she had written and sent to me
on that Easter morning (a morning which
must ever shine out white and fair in my
memory) when she and I had knelt side by
side after confirmation to take our first communion. I remember that she called them
" This Only," and had headed them with the
words, "Why call ye Me Lord, Lord, and
do not the things which I say ?"

"O feeble lips that lapse from fervent prayer,
  To smile at sin, and lightly laugh at shame,
That in the chamber loud your love declare,
  And in the world scarce dare to breathe His name,
    Whence would *ye* call Him Lord?

"O changeful soul! now mounting like thin fire,
  Skyward and Godward; now like thing of night,
Low-grovelling, smirched, and mid foul mud and mire
  Trailing white pinions given for starry flight,
    Darest *thou* call Him Lord?

"O morning's hope! O evening's dull despair!
  O lofty purpose! puny, paltry deed!
O high resolve! heart big with longings fair!
  O loveless life that bears nor flower nor seed!
    Dare *ve* to call Him Lord?

"Yea, I would call Him Lord, and all the more
  For this my sin, else were I sore undone;
Say, who should seek Him, if not I?  He wore
  This fleshy garb, yet in Him sin was none,
    So may I call Him Lord.

"No heaven I ask, no crystal-shining shore,
  Nor realm of flowers—this only would I pray,
That mid all sinnings, stumblings sad and sore,
  I still may cling to Thee, dear Lord, alway,
    And still may call Thee Lord."

M

She ended, and as her voice died away into a whisper sweet and low as the restful ripple of the rain, I hid my head between my hands and sobbed aloud, for something there was in the words and in her way of repeating them, which carried me back in thought to that vanished season of Youth and Hope when pictures and poetry, flowers and music, as well as sunrise, sunset, and the play of evening light upon the sea, had seemed but as the visible embodiment of my own thoughts, and were indeed to me as a part of my aspiration towards a loftier, lovelier life.

And then I remembered what manner of man I was, and as the shadow-horror of my sin arose spectre-like between myself and my distant childhood, I saw that "little brother," the child that I once had been, shrink back and back with sad reproachful eyes, until with a sudden cry of anguish and despair he turned from me, and fled into the night.

# CHAPTER XIII.

## *A DREAM OF ETERNAL REST.*

"DO you see that young man with the dark, delicate features?" she continued, giving an unexpected turn to the conversation. "I mean the one with the brown eyes that have so strange a look in them. He is a poet, and when he was on earth he was blind, but his songs were sad as the sighing of the wind in the pine trees, and sweet with sound, and perfume, and the love of woman. He and I were then, as now, the most devoted of friends, and it was our custom to spend one evening at least in each week together. Sometimes

we talked of places or of pictures (in both
of which, notwithstanding his blindness, he
took a singular interest), sometimes of poetry
or flowers. Not seldom he would sketch
out for me the plot of some story he was
writing, and often I would read aloud while
he sat listening with tranquil face and closed
eyes in his accustomed place by the fireside.
I remember that on one occasion the piece
which we thus read together was Jean Paul's
Dream of the Dead Christ saying there is
no God, and that when next I saw my poet-
friend, he told me that after I had left him,
he had fallen asleep, and dreamed a dream
which he spoke of as 'the most impudent
piece of plagiaristic imitation which ever
was perpetrated,' and which he called his
'Dream of Eternal Rest.'

"'As I sat here in the darkness which has
now become to me like a house of which I

am the only tenant,' he said, 'I fell asleep
and dreamed that I saw my life lying behind
me like the line of phosphorescent light
which marks the track of a fallen star—a
line traced in darkness, and which arising in
darkness dies away into darkness again; and
in my dream an angel appeared unto me,
and, laying his hand upon my shoulder, said,
" Thou who probest the mysteries of life,
and peerest into the time which is to be,
arise, come with me, and I will show thee
something of that which thou seekest."   So
saying, he stretched forth his hand, which
I clasped, and we set forth on our infinite
journey.

" ' What abysmal realms of space we
passed I know not, for I was as one bewildered by the swiftness of our flight and
by the rushing beat of the angel's pinions.
I remember that ever and anon there swam

up in the darkness a gleam of light that was
at first no bigger than a single star, but
which, as I looked, loomed out ever larger
and larger, and each moment seemed to
double in magnitude, until I trembled lest
it should break the bounds of the heavens;
but even as I trembled, it swept whirling by
with a sound like that of infinite thunders,
and, receding again, lessened before my eyes
as visibly as it had increased, and finally
dwindling to a mere point of light, died away
into darkness.  Ere long, however, there
appeared a flush in the distant east, and as
we drew nearer I saw that, below me and
afar, there lay a land in which the sun shone
with such exceeding splendour, that the at-
mosphere, light-filled and luminous unto
sparkling, was in colour like unto the colour
of a rainbow.  And I saw also that the rays
neither dazzled nor scorched, as do the rays

of the earthly sun.   And far as the eye
could reach stretched shining hills, seen
through soft vistas of purple and gold, and
sunny meadows wherein bloomed flowers
beautiful as the blush of a maiden, and
pure as an angel's thought.   And winding
in and out among the meadows ran many a
rippling river; and fountains also I saw, the
waters of which, as they rose and fell scin-
tillating like a shower of starbeams or spray
of diamonds, discoursed music sweeter than
the sighing of Æolian harps.   Then as I
looked yet closer, I saw, wandering hand in
hand among the meadows, many white-clad
figures, whereat my soul wept for gladness;
and I turned to the angel saying, "Surely
this is that Heaven whereof we read and
wherein I would rest for ever? for I am
sore wearied with the toil and the labour of
earth."   But he answered me, "Mortal, thou

knowest not what thou askest. Lift up thine eyes, and see if thou beholdest aught else."

" 'And I looked to the right hand and to the left, yet saw I only the sunny meadows and rivers of the land of flowers, and the blue distance of the bordering hills. Then I turned me round and gazed whence we came, but could nothing discern save remote plains of darkness, athwart the gloom of which I saw flash ever and anon (as one sees flash the eyes of a beast at midnight) the glimmer of a moving world. Then the angel stretched forth his hand, pointing me yet again to the distant east, and far away beyond the beauteous realm I beheld a vast plain of desolation, and beyond that a land whereof I could nothing see, save that a darkness, as of a twilight in which there is no moon, brooded above it like a cloud.

" 'Whereat a shuddering horror seized me,

so that I could look no more, and turning
to the angel, I said, " Alas! lieth the region
of endless night so nigh unto the realm of
eternal day ? "   But he answered me sternly,
" Mortal, thou speakest that of which thou
art ignorant.  Come, let us go thither, that
thou mayest see, and seeing, learn."   And
I cast a longing look upon the beauteous
land, and, lo! on the faces of those who
walked therein, I saw a shadow as of something incomplete—not discontent, neither
sorrow nor care, but the look as of an
unfulfilled aspiration ; but, even as I gazed,
the angel smote the air with eagle pinion,
and I beheld no more until we came nigh
unto our journey's end.   Then, every stroke
of his wing bringing us nearer, he turned to
me, once again bidding me " See, and seeing,
learn," but at my heart lay such a nameless
terror that I was as one spell-bound, and

durst not look upon his face. And with trembling voice I made answer, "Suffer me rather to depart, I pray thee! for I would not that mine eyes should behold the horrors whereof I have heard, and my soul longeth to return to the land of flowers wherein they toil not, neither sorrow, and where I shall cease from labour and be at rest."

"'But for the third time he bade me "See, and seeing, learn;" and as I looked upon the land which lay below me, I saw —instead of the realm of endless night— a shining city of such unimaginable beauty, that my heart sank within me in breathless awe. Then the angel spread forth his wings still and motionless, and we reposed on the azure air as a planet floats upon the purple bosom of night; and though neither sun nor moon was set in the peaceful heaven, I saw that there rested over

the city the soft splendour as of a world of
far-off stars. There was but one gate, and
over that was written in letters of light, "*My
Father worketh hitherto, and I work,*" at
which I marvelled exceedingly; and inside
the gate walked beings of such divine
dignity and soul beauty that I could have
knelt worshipping before them, were it not
that they too were of human form and
feature; and I saw that all were earnestly
but unhastily engaged in some manner of
work, at which they toiled serenely. And
on every forehead was set the seal of a high
purpose, and over the city there rested the
calm of an immeasurable peace. Then
silently upstole in the sky the dawnings of
a great light, deep and wide as the infinite
of Heaven, and athwart the glory thereof
there spread the fore-splendours as of the
approach of an AWFUL PRESENCE.

"'And around me fell a darkness like unto midnight, and, turning to me yet again the angel said, "Mortal, thou mayest behold no more. Return to thy home and to thy labour, never more to murmur or complain, and when thou longest after the repose of the world to come, know for a surety that there is no rest either in earth or in heaven, save in the fulfilment of the work which God would have thee to do;" and so saying, he too passed away into the darkness, and— I awoke.'"

"That is a singular dream," I said, "although it was scarcely necessary to have mentioned that your friend had been making a study of Jean Paul. But I suppose there really *is* work to do in Heaven?"

"It is very much as it is on earth in that respect," she answered, "excepting that here one loves one's work, and, although

here too, there are alternate periods of
labour and repose, it would be difficult for
some of us to say which is the sweeter. I
could tell you which *I* love the more, but
then all our work is of our Father's ordering,
and He knows just what is best for each
of us. Some who come here (never mind
my smile! I was thinking of the 'tired
woman' who was 'going to do nothing for
ever and ever') have to take a very long
holiday before they are allowed to put hand
to anything; and others there are whose
first task it is to learn those lessons which,
through unfavourable circumstances or the
accidents of their birth, it was hardly to be
expected they could have learned on earth.
There are some of the poorest of the poor
in East London, among whom by our
Father's direction I am now working, who
I believe have had scarcely more oppor-

tunity of knowing what Christianity means
to them than have the very heathen. Some,
when they come here, have to start from
the beginning, so you can believe that for
you who can write, as well as for those
who can preach, there is every opportunity
for the exercise of God's gifts—only remember!" she added sadly, but with a smile,
"that the popular preacher of earth, be he
poet or parson, is not always the man who
can do most good in heaven, for here one
is expected to practise as well as to preach."

"So you are entrusted with the task of
ministering to certain of the poor in East
London?" I said; "I had no idea that our
Father permitted those who had once left
the world to return to it again."

"Half of our work, and more, is on
earth," she made answer. "It was to tell
you of that that I pointed out my poet-

friend, the dreamer of dreams, to you.
Himself a poet, he was the son of a poet,
who had lived to see all else he loved on
earth pass away before him; and when this
boy, his darling hope and only companion,
was also taken, the old man was left lonely,
desolate and infirm. But not so lonely as
one might imagine, for his boy seldom
leaves him, and the work which God has
set apart for the poet-son, and which is to
him the resting-work of heaven, is to be
with his father in all sorrow, to minister
to him in all pain, and to be with him in
every wakeful or weary moment, his unseen
comforter and friend."

I was interested in what she related, for
I remembered that when I was sitting one
evening with the poet-father, he had told
me that, for all his loneliness, he was never
alone. "No, I am never lonely," he said,

"although you will perhaps think what I am going to tell you is but an old mans' fancy. A night or two after my dear boy died, I was thinking of my dead youth, and of my dead wife, of my dead friends and my dead children, until it seemed to me as if I, too, ought long since to have been buried, for I was lingering on (like a spectral moon when the sun is high) the living ghost of a vanished past. The generation had departed which I knew, and the one which was growing up around me was too busy listening to the songs of its own singers to give ear to mine. As the thought of my loneliness, my loveless life, and my boy's newly-made grave, away out in the dreary cemetery, came over me, I did that which was cowardly and faithless, and dropped my head upon my hands and wept. Then it was that there came a touch upon my arm,

N

and a voice in my ear, and though I knew none else was in the room, I was not afraid, but answered without looking up: 'Who is it?'

"'It is only I, dear father,' the voice replied, 'only your boy. You must not be unhappy about me, for though I have greatly sinned, yet I have been greatly forgiven, and am perfectly, peacefully happy.'

"My son then went on to tell me," the old man continued, "that for me there was to be no more loneliness, for that in all my sleepless nights and sorrowful days, he would be with me ever and always, my constant companion and comforter, until for me too the time shall come when,

"'Midnight waking, twilight weeping, heavy noontide
  —all are done.'"

＊          ＊          ＊          ＊          ＊

"That is a very touching incident," said my friend, when I had related this conversation to her. "If all earth-dwellers were as spiritually-minded as yonder poet's poet-father, and were as capable of apprehending how real a thing spiritual companionship may be, our dead would soon cease to be called our 'lost ones,' and death would no longer be spoken of as the 'great parting.' Death gives us more friends than he takes from us, and often brings us nearer to those who have gone before, than we were during their lifetime. Though it is nineteen hundred years since our Master, Christ, trod the earth a visible Presence, yet He is more to the world to-day, and nearer to each separate soul in it, than ever He was to the men and women who touched garments with Him when He walked the fields of Palestine. *Then* such as sought His aid had often to wait His coming in weariness and weakness of soul, whilst not seldom it happened that they could not obtain access to him 'because of the throng,' and we read even of one who was fain to climb a tree to catch a glimpse of Him in passing. *Now* He stands by each of us, waiting and willing to hear. *Then* they had to go to Him; *now* He comes to us, and is with us always and in every place. I tell you that Jesus Christ is as real a Presence to-day in the streets of London or Boston, as He was in the homes of Nazareth or Jerusalem. He is as near to us now as He was to Martha and to Mary, and is as willing to help and hear you or me, as He was to heal the sick, or to pardon the dying thief;" and then in a low, sweet voice she repeated the following lines from Whittier's poem, "Our Master":—

" But warm, sweet, tender, even yet
    A present help is He ;
And faith has still its Olivet,
    And love its Galilee.

" The healing of His seamless dress
    Is by our beds of pain ;
We touch Him in life's throng and press,
    And we are whole again.

" Through Him the first fond prayers are said,
    Our lips of childhood frame,
The last low whispers of our dead
    Are burdened with His name."

" The thought that the ' last low whispers '
of the loved ones who have left us were
' burdened ' with the Name which we first
learned to lisp at our mother's knee is a
very tender and beautiful one," she said
reverently, after a moment's silence. " We
seem to see our own fathers and mothers,
and their fathers and mothers, linked to ourselves, and through us to our children and
our children's children, until all the genera-

tions of the world—past, present, and future —become as one family in a great bond of fellowship, even as all the joy and sorrow of humanity find one common home in the heart of the Lord Christ who loves us."

" I am not sure that I realize this love of His of which you speak," I said sadly. " It is so vague and vast that I become lost, and feel that I have no personal hold upon it. How can He love the whole world, and yet love each separate individual in it with an affection as distinct as that which I feel for my wife and children ?"

"You cannot realize it as existing in yourself," she made answer, "although even you love all your children, and yet love each one of them with a distinct and personal love ; but then you cannot order the suc-cession of the seasons, or stay a planet upon its course, and you might just as well try to

measure God's power by your power, as try
to apprehend the love which passeth understanding by likening it to your own. But
you will know what Christ is to us one
day."

"Tell me more of Him," I whispered
eagerly; "tell me more of Him. Did you
love Him as earnestly and believe in Him
as trustfully when you were on earth as you
do now?"

"Not always," she answered sadly, "not always (and, oh! it was such 'cold comfort'—
the talk of the Pantheists and the Deists to
whom I had gone), but I came at last to see
that the Cross of Christ is humanity's only
hope. I came, too, to think that I could
better bear to disbelieve in a God at all than
to disbelieve in the Saviour. 'By Atheism,'
I said to myself, 'I lose only a Deity of
whom (excepting for the gospel-revelation)

I know practically nothing, but in losing
Christ I lose all—this world's hope as well
as the next's.'   There is not a creed which
has been offered us during the last eighteen
hundred years as a substitute for faith in the
Saviour which does not take the very basis
of its being from Christianity."

"Yes," I said; "but many people will tell
you that Christianity is nothing more than a
skilfully-framed fable, cunningly devised to
adapt itself to our human needs."

"Christ was, and Christianity was before
humanity or its needs came into being," she
made answer; "and the sacrifice of the
Cross was no afterthought given as a con-
cession to our human requirements.   On the
contrary, our human requirements were
given us that we, through them, might come
by way of Calvary to the feet of Christ;
and it is because it has been God's purpose

from all eternity to save the sinner by the sacrifice of Himself that you and I feel our need of a Saviour."

"Yes," I said, "I do indeed feel that whatever help comes to me must be something outside myself, and that no sorrowing of mine can atone for the past; but I feel also that I, and I only, am responsible for what I have done, and that to lay that responsibility upon another is utterly inadequate to satisfy even my limited sense of justice—besides which I never can and never will believe in the possibility of the innocent being allowed to suffer for the guilty."

"But the innocent do suffer for the guilty," she said, "even in the very earth-world, by the laws of which you wish to judge the heavenly one. You profess yourself willing to abide by the evidence of your senses, and if you will only look back upon the earth-life which you have left, you will see that the sins of the fathers are visited upon the children, and that the innocent are suffering for the guilty every day, and that God, for some good reason of His own, allows it to be so. As for what you say about your sense of justice, I agree with you that if a man run into your debt—run into your debt by wilful and wicked courses—he must be held answerable for the repayment of the money. But supposing one comes forward who loves him, and who has watched his sinnings with sorrow, and says, ' I will pay for my friend that which he cannot pay for himself,' would not your sense of justice be satisfied ? "

" Even then the moral obligation remains," I objected.

" Yes, but that obligation has been transferred," she said, "although as a matter of fact, it is against God rather than against man, that our blackest sins are committed. But, independently of that side of the question, Christ has taken the consequences of your sin, and of the wrong you did Dorothy—the consequences to her, as well as to yourself—upon Himself, and has suffered for you and for her in His own person, and if He be willing to forgive, then are you forgiven indeed!

"That reconciliation by the Saviour should at any time have been to me an intellectual stumbling-block is now beyond my comprehension," she continued earnestly. "In its very adaptability to our human needs, Christianity bears the stamp of its divine origin. Left to himself, the very best of us must feel his inability either to atone for the evil he has already done, or to with-

stand the temptations which yet await him
in the future, and though he struggle right
manfully to clamber out of the gulf into
which he has fallen, the dead-weight of his
sins, which he carries and must carry chained
log-like about him, is ever the heaviest clog
to drag him back.    But Christianity does
more for a man than merely forgive him his
debts.    It sets the bankrupt upon his legs
again, a solvent man and sane, with a clean
bill of health, and with a fresh start in life.
It is *the* religion of Hope, for none is too
sinful for the Saviour to save, and to the
man who brings his sins, as well as his
inability to resist his sins, to the feet of
Christ, there is indeed a present Help and
Hope in all his troubles !   There is much—
very much—in Christianity that I cannot
and do not pretend to understand, but I can
understand enough to make me very loving

and very trustful. The only mystery which still sometimes troubles me is that most terrible of all mysteries—the mystery of human suffering. But even that I am content to leave, for is not our God Himself a suffering God? and who that witnessed the sufferings of Jesus Christ (and what sufferings were ever like to His?) could have foreseen that the cruel Cross whereon He hung should hereafter be the finger-post to point the way to heaven? or that beneath His cry of agony in the garden, God heard the triumph-song of a ransomed world?"

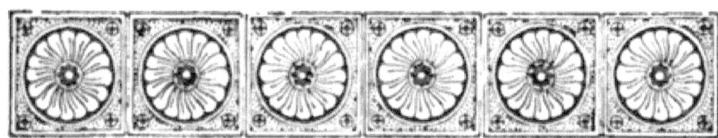

# CHAPTER XIV.

### *HOPE.*

AT last there came a time, even in hell, when the burden of my sin lay so heavily upon me, that I felt I could bear it no longer, and that if succour there came none, the very soul of me must wither away and die. It was not that I wanted to evade the punishment of my crime, for I was willing and wished to undergo it to the uttermost. No, that which was so terrible to me was the thought that not all the sufferings of eternity could avail to wipe away the awful stain upon my spirit, or to undo the evil which I had brought upon the woman I had ruined. Of myself and of my future, save for the continual crying-out of my soul after its lost purity, I scarcely cared now to think. It was of Dorothy that my heart was full; it was for Dorothy that I never ceased to sorrow, to lament, and—sinner, though I was—to pray. I saw then the inevitable consequences of the wrong I had done her pictured forth in all their horror. I saw her, with the sense of her sin as yet but fresh upon her, shrinking from every glance, and fancying that she read the knowledge of her guilt in every eye. I saw her, "not knowing where to turn for refuge from swiftly-advancing shame, and understanding no more of this life of ours than a foolish lost lamb wandering farther and farther in the nightfall," stealing stealthily

forth at dusk to hide herself from her fellow-
creatures.

I saw her, when the secret of her shame
could no longer be concealed, recoiling in
mute terror from the glance of coarse admiration on the faces of sensual men, or
shrinking in quivering agony from the look
of curious scorn in the eyes of maids and
mothers, who drew aside their skirts as she
passed them, as if fearful of being con-
taminated by her touch. And then—driven
out from their midst by the very Christian
women who should have been the first to
have held out a hand to save her—I saw
her turn away with a heart hardened into
brazen indifference, and plunge headlong
into a bottomless gulf of ignominy and sin.

Nor did the vision pass from me until, out
of that seething vortex of lust and infamy, I
saw arise the black phantom of an immortal

soul which was lost for ever, crying out unto God and His Christ for judgment upon the seducer!

\*      \*      \*      \*      \*

As these hideous spectres of the past arose again before me, I fell to the ground, and shrieked out under the burden of my sin, as only he can shriek who is torn by hell-torture and despair. But even as I shrieked, I felt that burden lifted and borne away from me, and then I saw, as in a vision, One kneeling in prayer. And I, who had cried out that I could bear the burden of my sin no longer, saw that upon Him was laid, not only my sin, but the sins of the whole world, and that He stooped of His own accord to receive them. And as I looked upon the Divine dignity of that agonized form—forsaken of His Father that we might never be forsaken, and bowed

down under a burden, compared to which, all
the horrors of hell were but as the passing
phantom of a pain—I saw great beads of
blood break out like sweat upon His brow,
and I heard wrung from Him a cry of such
unutterable anguish as never before rose
from human lips. And at that cry the
vision passed, and I awoke to find myself in
hell once more, but in my heart there was a
stirring as of the wings of hope—the hope
which I had deemed dead to me for ever.

*Could* it be—O God of mercy! was it
possible that even now it might not be too
late?—that there was indeed One who could
make my sin as though it had never been?
—who of His great love for Dorothy and
for me, would bear it and its consequences
as His own burden? and who by the
cleansing power of the blood which He had
shed upon the cross, could wash her soul

and mine whiter than the whiteness of snow ?

But to this hope there succeeded a moment when the agonized thought: "How if there be no Christ?" leapt out at me, like the darkness which looms but the blacker for the lightning-flash; a moment when hell gat hold on me again, and a thousand gibbering devils arose to shriek in my ear: "And though there be a Christ, is it not now too late?"

I reeled at that cry, and the darkness seemed once more to close in around. A horde of hideous thoughts, the very spawn of hell, swarmed like vermin in my mind; there was the breath as of a host of contending fiends upon my face; a hundred hungry hands laid hold on me, and strove to drag me down and down as to a bottomless pit; but with a great cry to God, I flung the foul things from me; and battling, beating, like a drowning man for breath, I fell at the feet of a woman, white-veiled, and clad in robes like the morning, whose hand it was that had plucked me from the abyss in which I lay.

# CHAPTER XV.

### HEAVEN.

IT seemed to me then that I fell into a sleep, deep, and sweet, and restful, in which I dreamt that I was a child lying upon the bosom of God. I remember that, as I lay, I stirred in my slumber, and, raising myself, chanced in opening my eyes to look below, but that with a cry of terror I turned and clung like a frighted babe to my Father's breast,—for beneath me and afar, there yet yawned the mouth of hell, from which, ever and anon, rolled dense clouds of hot and hissing smoke, that seemed to twist and writhe like souls in agony, and which in colour were like unto the colour of blood.

And I thought that, seeing my fear, my Father stooped to me as a mother stoops to comfort her frightened babe, and that as He stooped I beheld His face, and knew it for the face of the Lord Jesus, and that He bade me be of good cheer, "for underneath thee are the everlasting arms."

As He so spake I awoke, and saw that she whose hand had plucked me out of the abyss of horror into which I had fallen, yet knelt beside me in tender ministry and prayer, and that she was singing a hymn softly to herself whereof I heard only a verse :—

> " I know not where His islands lift
>   Their fronded palms in air ;
> I only know I cannot drift
>   Beyond His love and care."

She ceased, and I arose, but ere I had time to question her, I was conscious of a sudden stillness, like the hush which follows benediction after prayer. "Don't you hear it?" she whispered eagerly, as with upraised hand enjoining silence, she turned her head as if to catch some far-off murmur, "Don't you hear it? They are praying for you at home: kneel down!" And as her words died away, there seemed to float towards me the sound of air-borne music that stayed for one moment to fold me round with the sweet consolations of loving companionship and of peace, and in the next stole swiftly and softly away as if journeying onward and upward to the throne of God.

And with a great cry of anguish I fell to my knees and prayed: "O Lord Christ! I am foul and selfish and sinful! I do not

know that I love Thee! I do not know that
I have repented of my sins even! I only
know that I cannot do the things I would
do, and that I can never undo the evil
I have done. But I come to Thee, Lord
Jesus, I come to Thee as Thou biddest
me. Send me not away, O Saviour of
sinners. Amen."

As I ended, it seemed that my companion turned to leave me, and I fell to
sobbing and sorrowing, until at last for
very anguish I could sob no more. But
soon I heard again her returning footsteps,
and, looking up, I saw One who stood beside her, thorn-crowned, and clad in robes
of white. *His features were the features
of a man, but His face was the face of
God!*

And as I looked upon that face, I
shrank back dazed and breathless and

blinded;—shrank back with a cry like the cry of one smitten of the lightning; for beneath the wide white brow there shone out eyes, before the awful purity of which my sin-stained soul seemed to scorch and shrivel like a scroll in a furnace. But as I lay, lo! there came a tender touch upon my head, and a voice in my ear that whispered, " Son."

And as the word died away into a silence like the hallowed hush of listening angels, and I stretched forth my arms with a cry of unutterable longing and love, I saw that He held one by the hand—even she who had plucked me out of the abyss into which I had fallen—and I saw that she was no longer veiled. It was Dorothy— Dorothy whom He had of His infinite love sought out and saved from the shame to which my sin had consigned her, and whom

He had sent to succour me, that so He
might set upon my soul the seal of His
pardon and of His peace.    And to Him
be the praise.    Amen.

THE END.